Agatha ODDLY

THE SECRET KEY

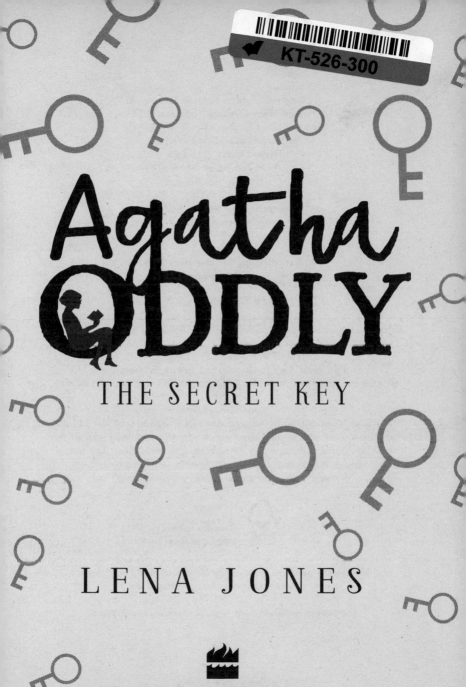

LENA JONES

HarperCollins *Children's Books*

First published in Great Britain by
HarperCollins *Children's Books* in 2018
HarperCollins *Children's Books* is a division
of HarperCollins*Publishers* Ltd,
HarperCollins Publishers
1 London Bridge Street
London SE1 9GF

The HarperCollins website address is:
www.harpercollins.co.uk
9

ISBN 978-0-00-821183-7

Typeset in Aldus LT Std 12/20pt by
Palimpsest Book Production Ltd, Falkirk, Stirlingshire
Printed and bound in England by CPI Group (UK) Ltd, Croydon, CR0 4YY

Agatha ODDLY

No case too odd . . .

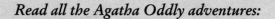

Read all the Agatha Oddly adventures:

THE SECRET KEY

MURDER AT THE MUSEUM

THE SILVER SERPENT

www.agathaoddly.com

For Kika and Mylo

1.

A LESSON IN CHEMISTRY

'This is the twelfth –' the headmaster glances up from his notes – 'no, let me correct that – the thirteenth time you've been in trouble this term, Agatha.'

We're sitting in his office, the air sticky, and that's not just because of the heatwave outside.

I look down at the floor. It's true, and I don't know what to say.

Dr Hargrave (Ronald Hargrave OBE, BPhil, MEd) likes to fill silences. He's very good at that, and it's best to wait until he's done. He isn't a doctor, as you and I think of them, but he likes to be called one. He has five liver spots in the shape of the constellation Cassiopeia on his forehead, and a steely glare, which I would say is a 4B on the eye-colour chart I have hanging in my bedroom.

He reads from his list:

'One – you were found hiding in the ceiling space above the chemistry labs, because you believed Mr Stamp was stealing sulphuric acid to sell on eBay.'

This really happened – he was – but without evidence I had to drop my investigation. Plus, Dad grounded me.

'Two – you tried to miss lessons by convincing the groundskeeper that you were an apprentice tree surgeon who needed to scale a tree near the boundary wall . . . and just so you could get out of school . . .'

I zone out. I've always found this easy – like switching channels on TV. If I want to watch something more interesting, I just imagine it. I call it my 'Change Channel' mechanism.

The headmaster's desk is very shiny and if I look down I can see my own reflection in the caramel-coloured wood. I'm wearing my red beret – Dr Hargrave hasn't even started lecturing me on this breach of uniform rules yet. My bob-cut hair frames my face, and my eyebrows are knitted together as though concentrating on his lecture. And, just like that, my reflection shimmers, shifts and becomes someone else. A small man in a hat and a bow tie looks back up at me. Smoothing out his moustache, he steps out of the desk, hops neatly to the floor and stands behind the headmaster.

'How long do you think le docteur Hargrave will go on this time?' he asks in a soft Belgian accent.

I zone back in to hear what my headmaster is saying now . . .

'Four – you installed a listening device in the wall of the staffroom . . .' – and then I glance back to where Hercule Poirot, famous detective, is looking at the clock.

'Your headmaster has already been talking for twenty-two minutes.' Poirot raises an eyebrow, as though daring me to do something about it. 'He might break his record of twenty-seven, no?'

Actually, I reckon the headmaster is almost done – his stomach just rumbled, and it's long after lunchtime. My eyes flicker around the room, details lighting up my mind like a pinball machine.

STOMACH RUMBLE

New haircut

Expensive Shirt – Silk

Chocolate – A gift

DARK GLASSES

'Twenty-four,' I say out loud.

'What?' The headmaster looks up from his notes.

'Nothing.' I clear my throat.

Poirot nods in recognition – I have made my bet.

'Are you listening to me, Agatha?'

'Absolutely, sir. You were saying that impersonating a health inspector is a criminal offence.'

'Yes, I was. Do you not take that *seriously*, Agatha?'

I nod seriously. 'I do, Headmaster. I was just starting to worry.'

'Worry? Worry about what?' The headmaster's eyebrows furrow.

'That you'd be late for lunch with your wife.'

A look of confusion creases his face at the change of tack. 'My . . . wife?'

'Yes. You're wearing a *very* nice shirt, sir. And aftershave. And I couldn't help notice the box of chocolates on your table, clearly a gift for a lady . . .' I smile, pleased with my investigatory skills.

'Aha, yes,' he splutters, 'my *wife*.' He looks at the clock on his wall. The words hover in the air like fireflies. 'As you were saying, I'm going to be late for lunch . . . with my wife.'

'Well, sir, I wouldn't want to make you late,' I say.

Dr Hargrave stands up, brushing invisible crumbs from his suit. 'Yes. I'd better get going.' He glances around, as though looking for the exit. 'As for you, Agatha, I would advise you to think about . . . um . . . everything I've said.'

'I will, sir.'

Dr Hargrave seems to be sweating as he shows me to the door where Poirot stands, smiling with approval. Poirot looks at his pocket watch.

'Twenty-four minutes – you were right, *mon amie.*'

I smile as Dr Hargrave opens the door for me.

'*Bien sûr,*' I say.

'What was that?' asks the headmaster.

'I said, enjoy your lunch, sir.'

He presses his lips together, as though holding something back, then mutters – 'Be careful, Agatha Oddlow. Be very careful.'

Liam Lau, my best friend, is pacing the corridor outside when I come out of the office. He turns to face me, his face all scrunched-up-serious. It takes me a moment to remember why. Ah yes – Liam knew I was in trouble and thinks I'm going to be expelled. In fact, Liam has been expecting my expulsion from St Regis since the day we met – only this time he's sure that this latest adventure will be my last. Wanting to draw out the suspense, I pull a sad face.

Liam covers his face with his hands. 'What did I tell you?' he wails. 'Who will I eat lunch with now?'

It's true, Liam and I do eat lunch together – every day, in fact – at least whenever we cross over after lessons. We sit on 'Exile Island' – the table in the refectory where all the weird kids sit.

'Liam . . .' I start.

'I know I shouldn't moan,' he groans.

'Liam . . .'

'Expelled . . .' He groans again. 'Oh, Agatha, maybe we can get him to reconsider? Maybe if we get your dad to write a letter—'

'Liam!' I shake him by the shoulders. Finally, he stops to listen.

'I'm not going to be expelled,' I say again.

He freezes. 'You're . . .'

'Not. E-x-p-e-l-l-e-d.' I spell the letters out, one by one, and examine my nails, painted forest green and bitten to the quick.

A smile smooths the worry lines from Liam's face. He grabs me and gives me a massive hug. 'What did Dr Hargrave say?'

I give him a sideways glance from under a fallen strand of hair. 'I'll tell you all about it. Come on – or we're going to be late for chemistry.'

'That's not a superpower.'

'I'm just saying – not getting expelled would be a pretty useful superpower.'

'But superpowers are stuff like invisibility, or levitation. "Not getting expelled" is just what normal people do.'

The school day is over, and Liam and I are meeting back in our form room.

'Normal people don't have as much fun as I do.'

Liam imitates the school librarian, looking disapprovingly over his glasses, and I can't help but smile. He always manages to cheer me up. He never judges me for Changing Channel, or for talking to people who aren't there. 'So, did you find any more clues about the caretaker?' he asks.

I shrug. That's why I was in trouble in the head's office in the first place – for dressing as a health inspector to check up on the caretaker who has been acting suspiciously for weeks. I've wanted to be a detective since I was young and love putting on a disguise. Mum always encouraged me. She liked setting me trails of clues to follow and solve. But, as you know, after several, ahem, *incidents*, I've been – well, I've been banned by the headmaster from doing anything that might be called 'snooping on innocent people'. Liam isn't as passionate about being a detective as I am, but he does enjoy solving puzzles and cracking codes. That's why we've set up the Oddlow Agency (no 'detective' in the title, to avoid annoying the headmaster).

'So shall we start the meeting, Agatha?'

'Yes,' I nod. 'I'll have to be quick, though; I need to get some stuff for dinner.'

'*Haute cuisine? Cordon bleu?*' Liam puts on an exaggerated French accent like I sometimes do when Poirot is with me.

'*Oui.* That's the idea, anyway.'

He nods seriously and opens the brand-new record book of Oddlow Investigations. My name is so often abused by other people (Oddly, Oddball, Odd Socks) that I've made it a part of my motto – 'No Case Too Odd'. Unfortunately, the Oddlow Agency hasn't been employed for a case yet. Still, that's no reason not to keep proper records.

'First order of business,' I begin, 'is the design of the insignia to be used on all official correspondence, business cards and rubber stamps. Any thoughts?'

Liam ponders for a second.

'What about a lion . . . holding a magnifying glass!'

Really? I give him a hard stare and change the subject. It doesn't sound very imaginative to me. 'Why don't we think about stationery later? We could practise taking identification notes?'

'Sure. But you'll have to tell me what *identification notes* are.' He grins.

I look across at him and smile. 'Identification notes are important facts about everyone. I write them for all sorts of people – anyone who might be important in an investigation.' I shrug. 'They help me remember what they looked like, how they dressed, what perfume they had on . . . that kind of thing.'

'OK, I reckon I can do that.' Liam nods. 'Let's start by giving it a go for each other.'

'OK, so take your notebook and write three identifying things about me. Things that are unusual – that make me stand out. I'll do the same for you.'

We put our heads down and scribble for a few minutes, then swap notebooks. Thoughtfully, I chew on my pencil as I hand them over.

My identification notes for Liam Lau –

1. Liam used to be smaller than me by a couple of inches, but has recently had a growth spurt that brings us level pegging.
2. He has black-rimmed glasses and dark hair, which is always immaculate. 'Geek chic' would describe his look.
3. He's inseparable from Agatha Oddlow.

Liam's identification notes for me –

1. Agatha is thirteen years old, 5 ft 2 (ish?). She has chestnut-brown hair worn in a bob.
2. She likes wearing vintage clothes – floral dresses, trench coats, DMs. So many trench coats. She's often writing in a notebook.
3. Always hanging out with Liam Lau.

I'm about to say that my hair is dark brown, not chestnut, when someone bursts loudly into the classroom.

'We can use this room, it's just Oddball and Boy Wonder in here,' they say.

I know immediately whose voice it is before I turn round – Sarah Rathbone, one of the three CCs, and she's got the other two with her – Ruth Masters and Brianna Pike. They say that CC stands for Chic Clique, but everyone else says it stands for Carbon Copies. With their identically blonde hair, manicured nails and primped and preened appearances, they stand for everything St Regis is about. The school is full of the rich and beautiful like them, and making the rest of us feel unpopular is what they're best at.

Some identification notes, for telling one CC from another –

1. *Sarah Rathbone – If the other two are copies, Sarah is the original. The jewellery she wears has real diamonds, but it's small and tasteful.*

2. *Ruth Masters* – Second-in-command, Ruth is ruder than Sarah, which is saying something. Her dad works in PR, and Ruth is just as conscious of her public image, carefully managing who the CCs talk to and who they avoid.
3. *Brianna Pike* – Brianna is Sarah's other henchwoman. She plays with her hair a lot and spends all day posting pictures of herself pouting on social media.

I face Sarah, head on. 'I'm afraid we're using this room,' I say.

'Using it for what?' Sarah sneers. 'Making detective notes with your little friend?'

Brianna approaches me. She draws her shoulders back and swings her blonde hair like a weapon. 'Move.'

'But we're in the middle of something,' I say.

'*We're in the middle of something?*' Ruth sing-songs back at me. 'Well, get in the middle of this – SCRAT.' She brings her face up-close-and-personal and I automatically spring back. She picks up the book I'm reading from the table – *Poisonous*

Plants of the British Isles – and shoves it into my chest.

'Enough messing around,' Brianna joins in, 'get out, Agatha. Get going.' She pushes my shoulder.

I brush my blazer as though some dirt has landed there. 'Come on, Liam,' I say, gathering my things. 'We're outnumbered.' And then I mutter under my breath, 'Physically, if not mentally.'

By the time the CCs realise they've been insulted, we've already left the room. The door slams behind us. I sigh, letting my frustration show.

'You OK, Aggie?'

'Yes . . . thanks, Liam.' I shrug. Sometimes I hate St Regis more than anywhere in the world. My first school, Meadowfield Primary, was so different. The buildings might have been falling down and there was never enough money for new books, but it had been bright and friendly, and the teachers had encouraged all of us just to get along. I had a nickname there – The Brain – which hadn't been a bad thing. It was a dumb nickname, but secretly I had liked it. At Meadowfield, being brainy was OK. When nobody

14

else knew the answer to a question, they'd turn to me. Then had come the scholarship to St Regis that my teacher had put me forward for. I *almost* hadn't shown it to Dad. When he saw the letter, he'd said it would be silly not to at least take the test. He'd been right, hadn't he? There was nothing to lose. Even if they offered me a place, I could still turn it down, right? And they probably wouldn't offer me a place anyway, would they?

I took the test.

I won the scholarship.

Dad sent a letter back, saying I would accept, starting in September.

I had been excited about going to a prestigious school at first. My new school had more money floating around than Meadowfield could have ever dreamed of. New computers, new classrooms, spotless walls and carpets. But in this place of shiny things, it was *me* who ended up seeming shabby. It didn't matter whether I was brainy. In fact, it didn't matter whether I was kind or funny or whatever else might have made me the person I was. I just didn't fit, until I met Liam . . .

I'd been sitting in the canteen (or *refectory*, as they preferred) of St Regis, eating lunch, when I pulled the *Sunday Times* from my satchel and started trying to do the cryptic crossword.

13 down – Calling for business meeting, talker gets excited.

'Perhaps "calling" means a telephone call.' A voice came from across the table. I jumped – I hadn't realised that I'd been thinking out loud. I looked up and saw a boy my own age who I recognised from class. His name was Liam Lau. I don't think I'd heard him speak once, except to answer 'present' when register was called.

'Sorry, did I startle you?'

'No, I . . . I just didn't realise I was talking to myself.'

He smiled. 'Do you do that often?'

'Maybe. Sometimes.'

'Me too.' He nodded, grinning. 'They say it's the first sign of madness.'

'Hmm . . . Maybe you're right about "calling" being a telephone call.' I said. Then, as though my brain had suddenly decided to co-operate – 'Oh, and what if "excite" means "jumble" – there might be an anagram in there?'

'Yes, that sounds good . . . Hmm, what about "meeting talker"?' Liam said. 'That's the right number of letters.'

We both stared at the letters M E E T I N G T A L K E R for a long moment. Then, together, we both shouted –

'Telemarketing!'

I was grinning as I took up my pen and put the answer in.

'Agatha . . .'

Liam's voice shakes me out of the memory. Here we are, almost a year later. I'm still a social outcast, but I have Liam as a friend. I look at him. 'Yes?'

'Promise me something?'

'What?' I ask.

'Try not to get expelled tomorrow?'

I roll my eyes. 'I promise.'

He grins. 'Come on, then – you can walk me to the bus stop.'

2.

HEMLOCK AND FOXGLOVE

I've just finished liquidising a pile of vegetables when Dad walks into the kitchen, begrimed with mud and smelling of manure. I'd forgotten my tiredness in the excitement of making something new.

'What on earth are you doing, Aggie?'

'Making dinner,' I say.

'With all the green mush, I thought it might be some kind of science experiment,' he laughs.

I sigh – Dad can be soooo closed-minded sometimes. He isn't a bad cook, but he isn't a very good one, either. I often make dinner for the two of us, but it's usually one of his favourites – something easy, like sausages and mash or beans on toast. Who can blame me for wanting to try something different for a change? I'd found a dog-eared copy of Escoffier's *Le Guide Culinaire* from a bookshop on the Charing Cross Road, and then spent an evening trying to decode his instructions from the original French. Dad looks over at the wreckage, shaking his head, and trudges off to get clean.

Dad – Rufus to everyone but me – has been a Royal Park warden since he left school at sixteen. He's worked his way up to the position of head warden of Hyde Park, so we live in Groundskeeper's Cottage. Still, even though Dad's in charge, he refuses to let others do all the dirty work and is never happier than when he's got his sleeves rolled up and is getting his hands dirty. He reappears in a fresh shirt, smelling strongly of coal-tar soap, which is an improvement from the manure. He looks over at the food I'm making, stroking his gingery-blond beard.

'What . . . is it?'

'Vegetable mousse, with fillets of trout, decked with prawns and chopped chervil.'

'Looks quite fancy, love.'

'Just try it – you'll never know if you like it otherwise.'

Dad shrugs and sits down.

I've been saving up for weeks for the ingredients. Dad gives me pocket money in exchange for a couple of hours shovelling compost at the weekend so it's been a hard earn. But it's worth it – everyone should have a chance to try the better things in life, shouldn't they? Dad reaches for his fork, staring at the plate. He searches for something diplomatic to say, and fails. 'It's not very English.'

I smile.

'Poirot says something like, "the English do not have a cuisine, they only have the food,"' I recalled.

He groans at the mention of my favourite detective. I go on about Hercule Poirot so much that Agatha Christie's great detective is a bit of a sore spot for Dad.

'You and those books, Agatha! Not everything that Poirot says is gospel, you know.'

I ignore this last comment and plonk a plate of

the fish and veg medley in front of him. He takes a fork of everything, and I do the same.

'*Bon appetit!*' I smile, and we eat together.

Something is wrong. Something is *very* wrong.

I look to Dad, and I'm impressed by how long he manages to keep a straight face.

Something awful is happening to my taste buds. I can't bring myself to swallow for a long moment, and then I force it down, gagging.

'I may have . . . mistranslated.'

Dad swallows, eyes watering.

'Might I have a glass of water, please?'

When the last of the mousse has been scraped into the bin, we go off to buy fish and chips. I decide not to paraphrase Poirot's thoughts on fish and chips, that 'when it is cold and dark and there is nothing else to eat, it is passable'. I don't think Dad would be amused and, besides, I really like fish and chips.

After carrying them back from the shop in their

paper parcels, our stomachs rumbling, we eat in happy silence. I savour the crisp batter, the soft flakes of fish, the salty, comforting chips. For once, I have to admit that Poirot might have been wrong about something.

While we eat, Dad asks about my day, but I don't feel like talking about school and the CCs, or the headmaster, or about how I'd zoned out in chemistry class, so I ask about his instead.

'So are the mixed borders doing well this year?'

'Not bad,' he grunts.

I think of the book I'm reading at the moment.

'And do you grow *digitalis*?'

'If you mean foxgloves, then there are patches of them down by the Serpentine Bridge.'

'What about *aconitum*?' I eat a chip, not looking Dad in the eye.

'Monkshood? You know a lot of Latin names . . . Yes, I think there's some in the meadow, but I wouldn't cultivate it. It's good for the bees, though.'

'Ah . . . what about belladonna?'

'Belladonna . . .' His face darkens, making a

connection. 'Foxglove, aconitum, belladonna . . . Agatha, are you only interested in *poisonous* plants?'

I blush a little. Found out! *Poisonous Plants of the British Isles* is sitting in my school satchel as we speak.

'I'm just curious.' Deep breath.

'I know that, love, I do. But I worry about you sometimes. I worry about this . . . *morbid fascination*. I worry that you're not living in the real world.'

I sigh – this is not a new discussion. Dad loves to talk about the REAL WORLD, as though it's a place I've never been to. Dad worries that I'm a fantasist – that I'm only interested in books about violence and murder. He's right, of course.

'I'll do the washing-up,' I say, quickly changing the subject. Then I look over at the sieves, pans and countless bowls that I've used in my culinary disaster. Perhaps not.

'My turn, Agatha,' says Dad. 'You get an early night – you look tired.'

'Thanks.' I hug him, smelling coal-tar soap and his ironed shirt, then run up the stairs to bed.

When we'd first moved into Groundskeeper's Cottage, I chose the attic for my bedroom. Mum had said it was the perfect room for me – somewhere high up, where I could be the lookout. Like a crow's nest on a ship. I was only six then, and Mum had still been alive. Before that, we'd squeezed into a tiny flat in North London, and Dad had ridden his bike down to Hyde Park every day. He'd been a junior gardener when I'd been born, still learning how to do his job. The little flat was always full of green things – tomato plants on the windowsills, orchids in the bathroom among the bottles of shower gel and shampoo . . .

The attic has a sloping ceiling and a skylight that is right above my bed so, on a clear night, I can see the stars. Sometimes I draw their positions on the glass with a white pen – Ursa Major, Orion, the Pleiades – and watch as they shift through the night.

The floorboards are covered with a colourful rug to keep my toes warm on cold mornings. We don't have central heating, and the house is draughty, but in mid-July it's always warm. It's been scorching today, so I go up on my tiptoes and open the skylight to let some cool air in. My clothes hang on two freestanding rails. Dad is saving to get me a proper wardrobe, but I quite like having my clothes on display.

On one wall there's a *Breakfast at Tiffany's* poster with Audrey Hepburn posing in her black dress. Next to her is the model Lulu. There's also a large photo of Agatha Christie hanging over my bed, which Liam gave me for my birthday. On the other is a map of London . . . Everything I need to look at.

My room isn't messy. At least, I don't think it is, even if Dad disagrees. It's simply that I have a lot of things, and not much room to fit them in. So the room is cluttered with vinyl records, with books, with a porcelain bust of Queen Victoria that I found in a skip. Every so often, Dad makes me clear it up.

And so, I try to tidy now. But with so little space it just looks like the room has been stirred with a giant spoon.

I take the heavy copy of *Le Guide Culinaire* and place it on my bookshelf, which takes up one wall of the room. I sigh – what a waste of time. What a waste of a day.

I run my hand along the spines of the green and gold-embossed editions – the mysteries of Poirot, Miss Marple, and Tommy and Tuppence – the complete works of Agatha Christie, who my mum named me after. She'd got me to read them because I liked solving puzzles, but said I should think about *real* puzzles, not just word searches and numbers. When I'd asked what she meant, she had said –

'Everybody is a puzzle, Agatha. Everyone in the street has their own story, their own reasons for being the way they are, their own secrets. Those are the really important puzzles.'

I feel hot tears prick the back of my eyes at the thought that she's not actually here any more.

'I got called in front of the headmaster today . . .' I say out loud. 'But it was OK – he just let me off with a warning.' I continue, tidying up some clothes. I do this sometimes. Tell Mum about my day.

I change from my school uniform into my pyjamas, hanging everything on the rails and placing my red beret in its box. What to wear tomorrow? I choose a silk scarf of Mum's, a beautiful red floral Chinese one. I love pairing Mum's old clothes with items I've picked up at jumble sales and charity shops, though some of them are too precious to wear out of the house.

Next, I go over to my desk in the corner and unearth my laptop, which is buried under a pile of clothes. I switch it on and log in. People at school think I don't use social media, but I do. I might read a paper copy of *The Times* instead of scrolling down my phone, and write my notes with a pen. But I'm more interested in technology than they'd know. You can find out so much about people by looking at what they put online. Of course, I don't have a profile under my own name. No – online, my name is Felicity Lemon.

Nobody seems to have noticed that Felicity isn't real. Several people from school have accepted my friend requests, including all three of the CCs. None of them have realised that 'Felicity Lemon' is the name of Hercule Poirot's secretary, or that my profile photo is a 1960s snap of French singer Françoise Hardy.

I scroll through Felicity's feed, which seems to be endless pictures of Sarah Rathbone, Ruth Masters and Brianna Pike. They must have flown out to somewhere in Europe for a mini-break over half-term. They pose on sunloungers, dangle their feet in a hotel swimming pool and sit on the prow of a boat, hair blowing behind them like a shampoo commercial. Despite myself, I feel a twinge of jealousy and put the lid down.

Rummaging through my satchel, I take out the notebook that I started earlier in the day. I put it by my bed with my fountain pen, in case inspiration strikes in the night – that's what a good detective does: they note down everything, because they never know what tiny detail might be the key to cracking a case.

Most of my notebooks have a black cover, but some of them are red – these are the ones about Mum – all twenty-two of them. They have their own place on a high shelf. My notes are in-depth – from where she used to get her hair cut to who she mixed with at the neighbourhood allotments. Every little detail. I don't want to forget a single thing.

I look over at Mum's picture in its frame on my bedside table. She's balanced on her bike, half smiling, one foot on the ground. She's wearing big sunglasses, a crêpe skirt, a floppy hat and a kind smile. There's a stack of books strapped to the bike above the back wheel. The police had blamed the books for her losing control of her bike that day – but Mum always had a pile of books like that. I don't believe that was the real cause of her accident. That's not why Mum died. Something else had to be the reason.

I climb into bed and pull the sheet over me, then take a last look at the photograph.

A lump rises in my throat. 'Night, Mum,' I say, as I turn out the light.

3.

THE SILVER TATTOO

'Dad, will you stop letting Oliver walk all over the work surface? It's unhygienic.'

I'm trying to wash up the bowl I used for breakfast, but our cat is sitting by the sink and keeps batting my hand with his tail. He's purring loudly at the fun new game he's invented. I turn to look at Dad, who is hunched over a bowl at the table. He shrugs and shovels in another spoonful of cereal. He's running late, as usual.

'I can't watch him all the time, Agatha.'

Sighing, I scoop Oliver off the counter. He's grey, and on the portly side from all the treats Dad feeds him.

He causes so much trouble, but he has a special place in my heart. He's middle-aged in cat years, and his main hobby is sitting – on the work surface in the kitchen, in front of the mirror in the hall or on the threadbare armchair that used to be Mum's. I suppose he misses her too. When he isn't sitting, he's lying down.

Oliver rubs his face up against my chin and I scratch the soft fur of his neck. I can feel his low, rumbling purr in my chest. I think back to the day I first met him. It was a rainy afternoon, and I was sitting by the fire, reading. Mum had come in through the front door with a cardboard box, which she brought over and set down in front of me.

'What is it?'

'Why don't you find out?' she said, smiling and shaking the raindrops from her hair.

I opened the wet cardboard box. At first it seemed to be full of nothing but blankets. I looked at Mum, puzzled.

'Keep searching – just be careful.'

I pulled back the layers of blanket, realising that there was a sort of hollow in the middle of them, like a nest. And there – curled into itself and barely bigger than my fist – was a kitten. My eyes widened with surprise, and I didn't dare touch the sleeping creature.

'Go on – you can stroke him.'

'Him?'

'Yes, he's a boy. You'll have to think of a name.'

I thought about this for a moment. 'Why do I have to think of a name?'

Mum laughed. 'Because he's yours.'

'He's . . . mine?'

Something like a shiver passed through me as he opened two huge ink-black eyes and looked up at me.

Then Mum had put her arms round me from behind and held me while I held Oliver. I closed my eyes.

⚷

The memory was so clear – even though that kitten was fully grown now, Mum was still somewhere behind me, holding her arms round me. He might have been mine, but his heart always belonged to Mum.

I put Oliver down on the tiles and clear my throat. As I finish my washing-up and dry my hands, Dad brings his empty bowl over to the sink.

'Are you OK, love?'

I nod and manage a smile. 'I'm fine.'

'It's just, you look a bit . . .' He puts his head on one side.

'. . . of a genius?' I suggest, trying to deflect the attention from myself and clear the lump in my throat, but he doesn't laugh.

'Is something wrong?' Dad is more interested in things that grow in soil than things that live in houses, but sometimes he notices more than I expect.

'I'm fine, Dad, really . . .'

'Really?' He puts a shovel-sized hand on my shoulder.

'Yes, really, Dad. Now go — get to work before you're late!' I reach up on tiptoes and hug him. For Dad, actions make more sense than words. He softens.

'Hold on,' I say, 'your collar's all twisted.' I sort out his polo shirt and he stands very still, like an obedient child.

'Right – you'll do,' I say, giving him a kiss on the cheek. 'Off you go.'

'Have a good day, love.'

Dad goes, and I rush back upstairs to finish getting ready. I brush my teeth and pull on my blazer, brushing my hair until my dark bob shines. I tie Mum's red silk scarf round my neck like a lucky charm and, finally, put on my tortoiseshell sunglasses – perfect for observing people without them noticing. Next, I pack my satchel – notebook, magnifying glass, sample pots for evidence, fingerprint powder and my second-best lock-picking kit. (My best one has been locked in the headmaster's shiny desk since yesterday afternoon.)

Outside, the sun is bright. Dewdrops sparkle on the emerald-green lawns and the sun fades. It's been hot today. I feel a swell of pride – the beautiful trees, the grass and flowerbeds, all lovingly tended by Dad and his wardens. I step through the wrought-iron gate of Groundskeeper's Cottage and close it behind me, taking my usual route along the Serpentine lake. I'm looking forward to my morning chat with JP, who lives in the park. JP isn't *supposed* to live in the park – he's homeless – but Dad pretends not to notice when he's still there at night-time. Dad says he scares off the occasional graffiti artist. This morning, as I approach, I see JP sitting with his eyes closed, looking pale.

'Hey, JP!' I hurry towards him. I have a premonition that he will fall forward as I reach him, a knife sticking out of his back. He would murmur something as he fell into my arms – 'Agatha, you must avenge me.' Then I would . . .

'Morning!' JP calls brightly, his eyes flicking open. He's not dead.

'Were you comfortable last night?' I ask.

'Not too bad. I slept under the weeping tree in the Dell. Don't tell your Dad, though.'

'Did you make sure not to leave a trace?'

'Not a fingerprint.' He laughs and eyes my pockets hopefully. 'Do you have anything to eat?'

I pull out two pieces of toast, sandwiched together with butter and marmalade.

'Thank you, my dear.' He takes a large bite, then speaks through a mouthful. 'Now, by the way . . .'

'Yes?'

'Don't you have a school to go to?'

I check my watch. It's 8:37 already; school starts at 8:55. 'Yup, I'd better run. Bye!' I set off at a brisk walk.

'Have a good day!' he calls after me.

I walk along the path. There aren't many people around at this time, but I nod to an old lady as I pass her, and she smiles back. She's walking fast, wearing a light tan coat and matching hat.

As I pass under the canopy of beech and willow trees, I hear a roar ahead. Approaching me, far too quickly, is a motorbike. Motorbikes are banned from the park, the same as any vehicle. I feel cross, but I have no time to react as the bike shoots past me, down the footpath and out of sight. A moment later and I hear a screech of tyres, a loud thud, then nothing.

Before I know it, I'm running back in the direction that I've just come from, and as I round a bend in the path I see what I feared – the old lady in the tan coat lying on the ground. The bike is next to her, but only for a second – the rider revs the engine and speeds away.

'Hey!' I shout after the rider, rather pointlessly. 'Stop!'

Of course, the bike does no such thing, and just disappears down the winding path. I rush over to where the woman lies on the ground. Her hat is askew, her eyes closed, and the contents of her handbag are strewn over the path.

I stand frozen for a second, stunned. I have to check myself – I haven't Changed Channel. This is not a dream. This is *really happening.*

'Are you all right?' I ask, and she opens her eyes slightly, but just looks blearily at me, then blacks out.

'Help!' I shout. 'Someone, help!'

There is hardly anyone around, but JP comes running over.

'We need to call an ambulance. I'll call nine-nine-nine,' I say.

'You have a mobile?' He sounds surprised.

'Well, of course,' I say, a little peeved. 'I'm just not glued to it all the time. We need to hurry.'

I reach into my satchel and take out the phone. I press the 'on' button, but it seems to take forever to power up.

'JP, could you go and see if there's a warden nearby?'

JP makes off across the lawns, the sole of one shoe flapping as he runs.

I turn my attention back to the woman. She looks almost too peaceful, and for a second I'm worried that she might have died while I was distracted.

My phone finally powers up; I call nine-nine-nine and ask for an ambulance. The woman keeps me on the line at first, asks about the lady's breathing and pulse. Her right arm is twisted oddly under her and looks broken. Carefully, I unbutton the cuff of her coat sleeve and find her wrist. Pressing my fingers to her skin, I find a regular – if rapid – pulse.

The woman on the end of the line hangs up, telling me the ambulance is about to arrive and I should make sure they can see me. Taking my hand away, I notice something unusual on the old lady's wrist – a tattoo of a key.

It's very simple – one long line and three short, like the teeth of an old deadlock. Dad has a dozen keys like that on a ring, which open the old iron gates and grilles in the park, but it seems a strange thing to have tattooed on your wrist, especially for an old lady. The handle of the tattoo key is a circle with a dot inside, a bit like an eye. It's outlined in white ink, which shines silvery on her dark skin. I start to put her scattered things back in her handbag, hoping to find a next-of-kin contact. There's lipstick, some mints in a tin, a pen, a large set of keys (none of which are deadlocks) and a purse.

There's no perfume in the bag, though I can smell that she is wearing some. I sniff again – I can't help it – it comes instinctively to me. A waft of vanilla, a hint of leather and carnation. *Tabac Blond*, first made by Caron in 1919. An expensive perfume.

Her clothes are plain, but her blouse has the feel of silk. The mother-of-pearl buttons might be plastic, but I'm not so sure. I look in the purse for a contact telephone number, but find nothing except several business cards.

Hydrology? What does that mean? 'Hydro' is from the Greek for 'water'. So, she studies water? Out of ideas, I go back to making sure she's comfortable. I don't risk moving her right arm, though it looks uncomfortable bent beneath her. But, as I fold my blazer and place it under her head, I spot something in her left hand. I don't know how I missed it at first. With a glance at her peaceful face, I gently prise her fingers open to find a piece of folded pink newspaper – a page from the *Financial Times*. Looking around to see if anyone is watching, I open it out.

It has the usual stories – mergers of electronics companies, CEOs getting millions of pounds in bonuses, a story about London pollution. Without thinking, I fold the paper and slip it into my blazer pocket. JP hasn't returned yet, so I'm left alone to watch over the professor. Somewhere nearby, a siren starts wailing. I have an idea – opening my satchel, I take out a small brown bottle, unstopper it, and wave it under her nose.

It was insanely difficult to find smelling salts in London chemists. Finally, a pharmacy on Old Compton Street had agreed to sell me some, on the condition that I leave my name and address.

After a moment, the professor starts to take deeper breaths, and coughs twice. She opens her eyes and looks at me. The sound of the siren is much louder now, and I can see the ambulance racing across the lawns towards us, churning furrows into the dew-soft grass. Dad won't be happy. It stops right next to us. The two paramedics jump out and start to tend to their patient.

'What's that you've got there?' A paramedic points to the bottle I'm holding.

'Sal volatile.'

He looks blank.

'Spirit of hartshorn?'

'What?'

I suspect the man of being a little slow.

'Ammonium carbonate with lavender oil.'

'Ah, *aromatherapy*. New age.'

I sigh. 'If you say so.'

They check the woman's pulse and breathing, and shine a light in her eyes to check for concussion. Then they apply a sling before loading her on to a stretcher. The one who called my smelling salts 'new age' asks me some questions about what happened.

'Hit by a motorbike?' He shares a look with his colleague. 'She's lucky not to be more seriously hurt.'

'Pretty unlucky to get hit at this time of the day in a park, mind,' says the other paramedic.

'Luck has nothing to do with it,' I say. 'This was deliberate.'

⌐○

I give the paramedics my home address and say I'm happy to talk to the police. I think about offering to ride with the professor to the hospital, but before I get the chance the ambulance leaves, and I stand there feeling as though I've woken from a dream. But this was no dream, and when I reach into my blazer pocket – yes! – there it is – the folded sheet of newspaper.

'Thank goodness for that,' I breathe. There is a strange tingle behind my eyes. In the spotless blue sky above me, clouds are starting to form. Not just any clouds – they are spelling out words.

HIT-AND-RUN   Strange Tattoo

HYDROLOGY

Newspaper Cutting

The clouds form and dissolve away just as fast. My heart is racing. I pick up my satchel and start to walk, replaying the events in my mind, and several images refuse to fade.

I think of the biker, whose face was hidden by the dark helmet. I think about the business cards from the Royal Geographical Society. And, most of all, I think about the key tattoo, in its silvery ink. I've never seen that symbol before. I pause – or have I? There's something at the back of my mind, just niggling away at me . . .

I stop, feeling frustrated.

I'm already late for school, so surely it can wait another minute. I sit down on a park bench and open my satchel, taking out my current casebook. I'm so excited; it might as well be the first one – this is a new beginning. I flip open the notebook to the opening page and cross out the details about the local shopkeeper's parking violations. I write the heading: 'Hit-and-Run – Hyde Park', underlining it a couple of times. Then I jot down some quick notes –

1. Old lady knocked down in Hyde Park. The path was wide. Was this deliberate? What could the motive be?

2. Her perfume was expensive, and she had an unusual tattoo (sketch overleaf). Something seems odd here – what is her story?

3. Business card says she is a member of the Royal

I look over all those exciting question marks for a moment, puzzling it over.

Something is afoot, of that I am sure.

⌐○

'So, you saw an old lady knocked down in the park by a motorbike, and now you want us to investigate?'

Liam is staring down at my notebook and frowning. We're in form class, before lessons. 'Don't people get knocked down all the time? What makes this one any different?'

I glance to the front. Mr Laskey is behind his desk, reading the newspaper, and it's hard to tell whether he's sleeping or not. The rest of 8C are chatting noisily, so there is little chance of our conversation being overheard. Still, there isn't much time to tell Liam everything that has happened. Brianna Pike, one of the three CCs, is sitting on the desk next to us, but she's too wrapped up with doing her make-up to pay us any attention.

'Not just an old lady getting knocked down,' I whisper. 'There was something funny about it. This didn't look like an accident. There were . . . unusual circumstances. *Comprenez-vous?*'

'You mean –' he glances around at our classmates before continuing in a whisper – 'you think someone might have targeted her?' He sounds more excited than normal about one of my cases.

'Exactly! And if you come with me to the Royal Geographical Society, I'll prove it to you.' I hold out the professor's business card.

He takes it and reads. 'Professor D'Oliveira, Senior Fellow, Hydrology Studies—'

'We need to get going – *now*,' I say, cutting him off. 'Time is of the essence.'

'Whoa, hold up! We've got school. What's the hurry?'

'I need to solve this before the police do.'

'But we have a maths test! And you almost got

expelled yesterday! Just wait till we're finished.' His voice is plaintive – Liam loves maths tests. He runs a hand through his hair, making it stick up at strange angles. I resist the urge to reach over and smooth it down. I catch the eye of two girls, who seem to be staring at Liam. That's been happening a lot lately, since his growth spurt. They scowl at me and I shoot them a sweet smile as they start whispering to each other.

I lower my voice. 'I'm going now. Are you coming or not?' I hiss. I draw my notebook back towards me across the desk and stare down at it, trying not to be influenced by the pleading look in his eyes.

He sounds strained. 'Erm . . . not.'

'All right. But you can still help out with something.'

He brightens. 'What?'

'On the woman's wrist, there was a symbol.'

'A symbol?'

'Well, a tattoo. I feel like I've seen it somewhere before. I need you to find out what it means.'

'Sure. What did it look like?'

'I'll draw it for you.' I take my fountain pen and

draw from memory the eye-and-key tattoo. 'I was thinking you could check Masonic symbols first, then alchemical, witchcraft . . .'

'OK . . . I'll scan it into my laptop and run some image-recognition algorithms to—'

'Yes, yes. Whatever you have to do.' I should have mentioned before that Liam is a computer genius. When he gets going about techy stuff, I have no idea quite when he'll stop.

'Right, I'd better be off then.'

Liam shrugs. 'You're going to be in so much trouble if you're caught, Aggie . . . Oh, wait! Hang on a sec.' He reaches into his bag and pulls out a black box, which he holds up to my mouth. 'At least if I'm here I can cover for you. Say "here".'

'Why?'

'Just do it.'

'Here.' I repeat into the box.

He takes the box away and presses a button.

Here, says the box in my voice.

'I can hide this at the back of the class and remote control it with my phone when they call the register.'

'Can't you just say "here" for me?'

'Do you think my impersonation of you is that good?' Liam raises an eyebrow.

'Point taken. Now, I *really* need to go!'

'How are you going to get out? They've already locked the gates.'

'Well, it's a Thursday, isn't it?'

'Yeah, so?' He looks blank.

I smile.

'Don't worry, I'll tell you later.'

━○

Getting out of form class is as easy as excusing myself to use the loo. From there on, things become complicated. When I woke this morning, my brain felt grey and heavy, like an old wash rag that needed wringing out. But now I'm full of energy, which is good – I'll need to be as awake as possible to escape St Regis.

I take the stairs down to the assembly hall, my footsteps echoing on the stone floor. I have three minutes before the bell goes and everyone rushes out of class. I make it past the biology labs, alongside the headmaster's office and into the Great Hall with its polished maple floor. This is where we have assemblies, and where we sit exams. Even though the hall is empty, I feel watched by an invisible presence, and not just from the dusty frames of St Regis' past alumni. I shiver and hurry on.

Creeping quickly over to the back doors, I hurry out on to the playing fields. I take off my red beret, crouch down, and start to run under the windows of the maths department, where students are still in form class. From an open window, I can hear one of Dr Hargrave's sermons on innocence and obedience.

'The rules are there to protect students from themselves. Stay within the rules, children, and you have nothing to fear . . .'

'. . . and nothing to gain,' I mutter, forging on.

At the end of the block, I stop and peer round the corner. The entire school is ringed by a three-metre-high wire fence, impenetrable with the tools I have on me (strawberry-flavoured eraser, 2HB pencil). The only way out is in disguise, and I'm looking right at one – between the sports teacher's hut and the door to the kitchens stand the half-dozen wheelie bins that are collected by the council twice a week.

I know Mr Harrison, the PE teacher, will be having a cigarette in the privacy of his hut before the first class arrives to collect their hockey sticks and basketballs. He's a creature of habit (full-tar, slim filter), and I'm relying on that. Smoke signals from the window support my hunch. Coast clear, I creep across the open ground to the bins and quickly look inside each of them in turn. All of them are full to the brim with tied-up rubbish sacks. What a pain.

Quickly, making as little noise as possible, I empty one bin, stashing the sacks in the space between the hut and the back wall of the school. I take off Mum's scarf and put it in my pocket – I don't want it getting dirty. For a second I hear a noise from the hut and freeze, but nobody comes out. The bin is empty. I peer in. There is a thin, brownish slime at the bottom, and a strong smell of rotten fruit. I sigh. With a last look at my polished shoes and my lint-brushed skirt, I start to climb in.

As I do, there's a sound of unlocking from the kitchen door. Quickly, I crouch down in the foul-smelling bin and shut the lid. I'm in warm, smelly darkness, but I can hear well enough.

'Oi, Charlie! You got anything else that needs chucking? I'm gonna put the bins out.' It's one of the kitchen workers.

'Yeah,' replied another voice, 'take these peelings.'

There are muffled noises and footsteps coming closer. I close my eyes and hope he doesn't pick the bin I'm in. A moment later, light floods in. I look up. A young, stubbled face peers at me, looking startled.

'Oh, hey, David!' I say cheerfully.

'Again, Agatha?' He does not seem thrilled to see me.

'Look, David—'

'Dave.'

'Dave, this is very important.'

'It was very important last time. I could lose my job!' He speaks in an urgent whisper.

'Look, this is the last time, I swear. Never again.'

He stares at me, unspeaking, then back to the kitchen, then at me again.

'Never again,' he says. 'And if you get caught, I didn't know you were in there, OK?'

'Sure.'

He dumps the bag of potato peelings on my head and slams the bin shut. If I weren't in hiding, I might have sworn. I spend another five minutes in cramped confinement, trying to shift the soggy bin bag from my head without making a sound. I hear Dave taking the bins around me, one by one, to the gates. I'm sure he's leaving mine until last, prolonging my discomfort. Finally, I feel my centre of gravity shift sideways, and we begin the bumpy ride to the bin depot. With a last thud, my journey is complete.

I wait a moment until Dave has time to go back inside the gates. A dribble of cold juice has escaped the bin bag and trickles down my neck. A shiver runs up my spine. With the bag on top of me, it's impossible to peek out and see if the coast is clear. Instead, deciding I can't put it off any longer, I spring out.

The bin depot is outside the school grounds, next to the H83 bus stop. A small old man flattens himself against the shelter in shock.

'Sorry!' I leap out of the bin and make off down the road at speed, slinging my satchel over my shoulder.

'Stop!' he yells 'You . . . you criminal!'

I shout over my shoulder, feeling the need to correct him.

'I'm not a criminal – I'm a detective!'

4.

RUN-iN

Away from the bus stop, I take out my notebook. Where to start? Hmm. First I should take another look at the crime scene – the longer I leave it, the more it'll be contaminated with litter from passing tourists. Time is of the essence. From Hyde Park I can then walk to the Royal Geographical Society – the base for Professor D'Oliveira – on Kensington Gore. My body is tingling, almost light-headed. What is this feeling, I wonder? Then I realise –

Adrenaline! I feel alive!

As I hurry back towards Hyde Park, I have to skirt round crowds of tourists on every corner, stopping to have their pictures taken beside red phone boxes. When I get to the park, I use my best subterfuge to keep out of sight of Dad's gardeners, most of whom will know me if they spot me.

I cross the grass, rather than taking the main paths, hiding behind trees and shrubs, and only moving when I'm sure the coast is clear. As I reach the scene of the hit-and-run, I take a quick look around. There are plenty of people, but there aren't any abandoned wheelbarrows or lawnmowers to suggest a gardener is nearby.

I'm hoping to spot a clue to the biker's identity, when I see something glinting under a prickly shrub and, with a quick look down at my already filthy skirt, get down on my knees and crawl towards it. At that moment, I hear Dad's voice, sounding sombre and far too close.

'It's very strange; I've never seen anything like it before. I'm wondering if it's connected to the water mains. Anyway, I've taken some samples.'

I don't hear his companion's reply, but two pairs of feet stop in front of my hiding-place.

'This mahonia has got far too leggy.' It's Dad's voice. 'We should look at that in the spring.' Again, his companion makes a quiet response. I concentrate on staying still. Then the voices move away, and I realise I've been holding my breath.

They haven't seen me.

I look at the object I crawled under the bush for, but it's just a chocolate wrapper. I crawl out, feeling stupid, and hoping nobody spotted me.

'Agatha!'

Crud.

Lucy, Dad's deputy gardener who looks after the plant nurseries, has spotted me. Luckily, Lucy always assumes the best of me.

'How're you doing?' She blows a lock of hair out of her eye.

'Good, thanks. Busy.'

'Yeah, tell me about it. I've got weeds coming out of my ears!' Lucy grins. 'Shouldn't you be in school?' she asks, the first doubt creeping in.

'Free period,' I lie. Lucy deserves better, but I can't risk her telling Dad.

She nods, as though this should have been obvious. 'Oh, I have something for you.' She fishes in her pocket and draws out a pencil. 'One for your collection.'

'Thank you – where did you find it?'

She shrugs. 'Just down the path here. Anyway, I'd better get on.' She waves her border fork and heads back to work.

I take a seat for a moment on the bench. I look at the pencil a while before dropping it into my lap as though I've been burnt. A pencil, lying on the path near where the hit-and-run took place? Perhaps it belonged to the professor!

Careful not to touch the pencil any more, I take a pair of tweezers from my satchel and use them to move the pen to a clear bag. Embossed in gold on the side are the initials 'A. A'. Not Dorothy D'Oliveira's pencil, it would seem. The fingerprints on the outside of the pencil might have been wiped away by Lucy and me handling it, but there could still be some on the grip. Perhaps the pencil was dropped by a tourist passing through the park, but at this stage I have to take it seriously.

Standing, I dust myself down. I pause – I have the sensation that someone is watching me. I look around and see –

A MAN JOGGING Wearing Headphones

Receiving Orders?

A Blonde Family

Looking At Map

HIDING A CAMERA? Woman With Child

Pushing Buggy

Listening Device?

None of them seem to be looking directly at me, but good spies are clever. They're able to hide what they're up to.

I inspect my clothing quickly. The knees of my navy tights are green, as are the elbows of my matching blazer. Far worse, there is a rip in my skirt. I must have caught it on the shrub when I crawled under it. This is my only school skirt and I wonder if I'll be able to mend it without Dad discovering.

But for now, I have more important things to think about – time to visit the Royal Geographical Society (RGS).

It takes me no time at all to get from the park to Kensington Gore. The exterior of the RGS is a bit disappointing – from the name you might expect a beautiful structure, like the white-and-redbrick façade of the Science Museum on the nearby Exhibition Road. The RGS entrance is a newer addition, made from floor-to-ceiling glass. It looks like it might take off in a strong gust of wind.

I walk the short distance from the pavement to the glass entrance. Inside, a man in a smart suit sits behind the reception desk. He looks me up and down – slowly, and with a raised eyebrow.

'Not looking your usual well-coiffed self today, Agatha,' he observes.

I pull a face and smooth my bob. 'Sorry, Emile. Difficult day. I was hoping to speak to you about this . . .' I draw the business card from my pocket.

'Agatha, we've been over this,' he interrupts, shaking his head. I feel quite sorry for Emile – he's always having to turn down my requests, and I can tell it doesn't suit him. 'I can't give you a lifetime membership to the Society.'

'Oh, no – that's not why I'm here.'

'It's not? You mean . . . you have a query – an actual query – that I might be able to help you with?' He brightens.

I nod.

'Oh, good.' He smiles. 'I have to say, I was surprised that you weren't wearing some disguise or another. Like that dirty jumpsuit!'

Ah yes – the time I pretended to be a plumber. 'Well, anyway . . .' I change the subject. 'If you could take a look at this business card – it belongs to one of your members.' I place the card on the desk, and he inspects it.

'Professor D'Oliveira. Why are you enquiring

about her?' He narrows his eyes. 'Is this one of your detective games?'

'I do not play games, Emile. I conduct investigations.'

'Right . . . Is this one of your *investigations*?'

I pretend not to notice the sarcasm. I like Emile; it's just a shame he doesn't always take me seriously. 'Possibly . . . I mean, do you know Professor D'Oliveira?'

'Of course. She spends a lot of time here – she's a highly regarded member of the Society.'

'Good.' I take out my notebook. 'Then perhaps you could tell me more about her.'

'Why?'

'Sorry?'

'Why are you asking this?'

I hesitate. It's hard to know how much to tell. I didn't want to give any information about the hit-and-run if the Society don't already know.

'I met her in Hyde Park, earlier today,' I say. This isn't entirely a lie – I did meet her – she had smiled at me, after all. I think quickly and add, 'and I thought she might make an interesting subject for our school newspaper.'

He smiles. 'I'm sure she would. I can arrange to make an appointment for you to interview her – only, I don't think she's been in today, but let me call her assistant.' He reaches for the phone.

'Oh – don't worry about that for now,' I say quickly. 'Perhaps I might have access to the Society's archives today to check out some facts?'

'That might be a problem. I don't think you've filled in an application form for access to the Foyle Reading Room?'

I shake my head. 'Can I do that now?'

'I'm afraid, for under-sixteens, we would need parental consent.'

'Really, Emile? Is there nothing you can do?'

'Well . . . I suppose I could put in a call to your school – obtain their permission, as it's for the school newspaper.'

'Oh! No, that's all right. I'll leave it for now. Thanks anyway.'

'Sorry not to be more help. Do give me a call

tomorrow – Professor D'Oliveira often has meetings, so we can sort out that interview soon.'

'Yeah, thanks, Emile.'

He calls to my back – 'Agatha!'

I turn with renewed hope, ready to be as charming and grateful as required. 'Yes?'

'Did you realise you have a twig attached to your hair?'

'Ah . . . no.'

I remove the twig and carry it outside. It's hot after the air-conditioning, and I'm just pondering where to go from here when suddenly a hand covers my mouth from behind. I'm yanked backwards, out of sight of the foyer building with my arm pinned behind me. A male voice mutters in my ear –

'You really are a meddling little girl, aren't you?'

Strangely, I feel a moment of relief that I hadn't been imagining it – I *was* being watched back in the park!

But relief gives way to panic. I struggle, but can't escape the tight grip. Thinking back to self-defence manuals I've read, I scrape my heel up his shin and stamp hard on his foot. He grunts in pain but doesn't loosen his hold.

'You're a regular little snooper, Agatha Oddlow.' His breath is warm and wet on my cheek. He smells of whisky and Chanel Bleu aftershave. A man with expensive tastes.

'Are you afraid?' he whispers.

I shake my head as well as I can.

'Well, you should be – and if you aren't afraid for yourself, how about that father of yours? What if he had an accident? Be a shame for you to wind up an orphan, wouldn't it?'

I try not to react – how does he know my name, and what does he know about Dad? How does he know my mum isn't alive any more?

'Where would you live if something should happen to him? That little cottage goes with the head gardener's job, doesn't it?'

I try to calm my breathing, and focus on his accent. It's Scottish, that much is obvious. I think back to the tapes I'd listened to in the library – *Accents of The British Isles* – spending hours with headphones, playing the voices over and over, until I was confident of recognising them all.

Edinburgh – No.

The Borders – No.

Fife – No.

It comes to me – the man is from Glasgow!

This small victory does nothing to help my situation. A shiver works its way down my back. My breathing – already awkward due to the hand across my face – becomes laboured, and I can hear the blood pounding in my ears, like ocean waves. He leans in again. 'You didn't see anything this morning in Hyde Park – you understand me? Nothing.'

A rag is clamped over my mouth, and I smell something like petrol fumes. Darkness starts to pull me under. Sight leaves me, then sound, then touch. The last thing that lingers is the chemical smell.

Then nothing.

5.

THE RED SLIME

Darkness.

There is a tiny light, far off and I move towards it, but moving *hurts*. I'm not sure what is hurting – I don't have a body yet. Slowly the light grows, white in the darkness. I remember my body – legs and torso, arms and head. Ah yes, my head – that's where it hurts. I must have fallen. I can hear voices. Where is the man who attacked me?

'What's wrong with her?'

'Mum, is she going to die?'

'Has anybody called an ambulance?'

I lie there, breathing deeply for a while, wishing

for silence so that I can think straight. Another voice, gentle but firm, cuts through the rest.

'Excuse me, please. I'm a doctor.'

Then something soft is placed under my head. The white light fades and turns into a face – the face of a man.

'Hello. Are you all right?'

'Mmf,' I say.

'Let me help you up.'

The man takes my arm gently and helps me into a sitting position against the wall. The crowd moves away. As my vision clears, I look at the man who is crouching to help me. His hair is white, though he can't be much older than Dad. He has high cheekbones and very pale blue eyes. One hand grips a black malacca cane. His suit is white linen, with a silver watch chain between waistcoat pockets. His face is angelic.

'Are you all right?' he asks again.

'Yes.' I frown. 'I, uh . . . I'm fine. I just slipped,' I lie. My voice is hoarse – I haven't had a drink in ages, and my throat is dry and gritty. I look round, trying to pick out anyone who might have been my attacker. 'Are you a doctor?' I ask the man.

'Not practising. In my youth, I studied medicine at La Sorbonne.'

'Oh . . . Paris.' I say rather dumbly. My brain is full of fog.

He smiles indulgently. 'Now, do you feel up to standing?' He stands carefully, using the cane as support, and offers his hand. I take it, and manage to get to my feet, though my legs still feel wobbly. He's wearing cologne, but this time I don't recognise the brand. He's so elegant, so very well dressed, that I can hardly believe I'm awake at all. I feel so foolish standing in front of him – with a torn skirt and messed-up hair – that I can't think of anything to say.

'Are you all right?' He asks again.

'Oh, yes . . . thank you.'

'Not at all. Now, it's a hot day – I think you should get yourself a cold drink.' He takes a coin from his pocket and presses it into my palm. 'Doctor's orders.'

Smiling, he bows his head once and sets off down the street, malacca cane tapping the pavement. I feel a pang as he goes – as if an old friend has visited, but can't stay.

Dazed, I find my way across the street to the nearest pub, the Sawyers Arms. At least I'm not far from home. The inside of the pub is cool and dark, though the barman looks less than pleased to see me. Children aren't usually allowed in London pubs unaccompanied, but I'm desperate. I want to look for evidence outside the RGS, to track my attacker down. But I'm too tired, too thirsty.

'Can I have a glass of water, please?'

'We don't serve *kids*,' he says.

'Actually, under article three of the Mandatory Licensing Act, you're obliged to *ensure that free tap water is provided on request to customers where it is reasonably available.*'

A man sitting by the bar chuckles, but the barman only scowls more.

'On request to *customers*,' he says.

'Oh, let her have a drink, Stan.' The man on the stool says. 'It's as hot as brimstone out there.'

The barman grunts.

'Only if she buys something.'

'I'll have a packet of peanuts then,' I chip in.

The barman slouches to reach a pack and throws it in my direction. He gets a glass and picks up the nozzle, which dispenses fizzy drinks and water. But, when he presses the button, nothing comes out. He shakes the nozzle and tries again, but only a dribble appears.

'Damn thing . . . you'll have to have bottled.'

I sigh and hand over the money, too tired to question the charade.

I leave the pub, blinking in the sun's glare off the pavement. The road is so hot that the tar is melting – I can smell it. The air shimmers. My legs still feel shaky, but I have no money left to get a bus. I tell myself that I'm nearly home – all I have to do is get through Hyde Park without Dad spotting me.

It's weirdly quiet as I walk past the townhouses on Kensington Road. The air is thick with car fumes, and no breeze stirs. Far off, I can hear the siren of a fire engine. There is the usual row of tourist coaches opposite the park, engines idling to keep their air-conditioning going. At Soapy Suds, the carwash that cleans the Jags and Bentleys of Kensington, a man in a suit is arguing loudly with the attendant.

'Whaddya mean, you're not washing cars? Can't you read your own sign?'

Hyde Park is looking lush, even after weeks of heat – the lawns are emerald green, the flowerbeds blooming. Still, it seems too quiet for a summer's day in central London – just the occasional dog walker idling their way along a path. Have I missed something while making my investigations? Is everyone indoors, watching a major sporting event, perhaps? An ice-cream van drives past, blinds pulled on the serving window, chimes switched off.

I try to make sense of it, to shift my brain into puzzle-solving mode, but the same two words keep repeating in front of me, like a flashing warning sign –

TOO QUIET

I'm walking over the lawns towards Grounds-keeper's Cottage when I spot two figures in the distance. One of them is Dad, dressed in his overalls. The other man stands next to a large motorbike, and is wearing black biking leathers. His face is obscured by a helmet, but I can tell that the two of them are arguing. Before I know why, I'm running. The words of the man who grabbed me outside the Royal Geographical Society start to run through my head on a loop –

Be a shame for you to wind up an orphan, wouldn't it?

There is a knot in my stomach, like the end of a rope that links me to Dad.

Be a shame for you to wind up an orphan, wouldn't it?

I'm getting closer, and I can hear their raised voices. Dad lifts his hand, pointing towards the park gates. The man in black reaches back, towards the bike. The bike looks like the same one that knocked over the professor this morning.

Be a shame for you to wind up an orphan, wouldn't it?

In a fluid motion that makes my heart skip a beat, the man in black mounts the bike, kicks the machine into life and roars off, back wheel spraying clods of dry earth. Dad shouts after him, but he's drowned out by the roar.

'Dad, are you OK?' I yell, running headlong into his arms.

'I'm fine, I— Agatha, what on earth are you doing here?'

'Are you sure he didn't hurt you?' I step back to look at his face.

'Hurt me? Of course he didn't hurt me – I was just telling him he couldn't ride that stupid bike in the park. He's made furrows through the lawns, look. Anyway, don't change the subject – I got a call from your headmaster earlier. He said that you hadn't shown up for any of your classes today. He used the word *escaped*.'

Bother.

I swallow. In my moment of fear, I'd forgotten that I was supposed to be avoiding Dad on my way home.

'Ah, yes . . . about that . . .' I say.

🔑

Dad has given me some big lectures before, but this is the biggest. Being dressed down in public, as dog walkers pass by, is the worst. By the time he sends me home, with an order to go to my room, my cheeks are burning. I trudge back to the cottage, tired and miserable. His final words are the ones that sting the most –

'You're not a detective, Agatha. You're a thirteen-year-old schoolgirl. And if you carry on like this, you won't even have a school to go to!'

I'm angry with him for saying that, but he's right, isn't he? I'm not a real detective, and I've put more than my grades at risk today. Who the man in black was, I'm not sure, but I know I don't want to be that scared for Dad's safety again. Perhaps it's time to forget about investigating crimes.

As soon as I step through the front door, Oliver is mewling and winding figures of eight round my legs. 'All right, all right, hang on . . .' I mutter.

I dump my satchel in the hallway and go to the kitchen cupboard to find a tin of Yummy Cat Duck & Heart – Oliver's favourite meal, and the smelliest in the range. His mewls go up a semitone as he races between me and the food bowl. I dump the jellied meat in the dish, trying not to breathe too deeply. He eats happily for a few bites, then breaks off and starts mewling again.

'Thirsty? Me too . . .'

I pick up his empty water dish and take it to the sink. Again, Oliver is doing laps round my legs. I turn on the tap, and for a second nothing comes out. Then there's a dribble of water, a splutter, a choke, and suddenly something that *definitely isn't water* is oozing from the tap. I take a step back in shock and watch as thick red slime fills the sink.

The gloop isn't smooth, but rough like porridge, and the colour of blood. It's as though the sink is filling with fresh gore. It's so thick it can barely go down the plughole, spluttering and coughing bubbles of gas. And what an awful gas it is – suddenly the kitchen is full of a sickly stench. It's like the rotten smell of the bin I used to escape school – but worse. Whatever the stuff is, it smells dreadful.

Coming to my senses, I rush back to the sink and

turn the tap off. The stuff just sits there, refusing to drain. I take a fork from the drawer and prod it. Oliver, who at first continued crying for water, catches the foul smell and retreats to the doorway, from where he glares at me.

I bend over the sink to take a closer look, stirring through the red sludge with my fork. Bubbles blossom on its skin, so thick that when I prod them, they don't pop, only deflate. Suddenly my eyes are burning, and I start to choke. The air in the kitchen is full of fumes.

Quickly, I open the windows, then scoop the protesting Oliver and take him out to the back garden. As soon as I put him down, he runs across the lawn and leaps over the back fence. Outside again, the eerie silence covers London like a blanket. Far off there are sirens and a helicopter circling. In spite of myself I'm scared. I need to think.

After a little while has passed, I go back into the kitchen. The air has thinned out and doesn't burn my eyes any more, but the smell lingers. Most of the slime has oozed its way down the drain by now, and I wash the remainder away with a pan of rainwater fetched from the barrel in the garden. Then I go and turn the TV on, flicking through the channels.

'. . . Reports are coming in from as far west as Twickenham . . .'

'. . . People are advised not to run any taps or flush any toilets . . .'

'. . . Downing Street has yet to comment, but sources close to the Prime Minister say an emergency meeting of COBRA has been called . . .'

The newsreel shows people in protective suits going down into the sewers; people carrying buckets of red slime from their homes and tipping them down the drains; the head of the army holding a press conference near a water-pumping station. Then a man who looks vaguely familiar comes up on the screen. Just as he's about to start talking there's an explosive sound as Dad kicks the front door open. He's wearing an enormous pair of fishing waders, covered in slime. His eyes are pink.

'Dad! Are you OK?'

'It's in the Serpentine . . . full of it . . . bubbling up from nowhere . . .'

'Oh no!' I rush to help him.

'Don't! This stuff burns, whatever it is. Just put some newspaper down.'

'Dad, are you crying?'

'It's just this stuff. Stings the eyes. Come on – newspaper!'

I hurry off and find an old copy of *The Times*, spreading enough of it for Dad to get through the house to the back garden. Dad stomps through the house, already taking off the waders. As he swears and kicks the ground outside, my attention wanders back to the TV screen – the same pictures going around: people being interviewed, people going down into the labyrinth of tunnels beneath the city. It has spread from one side of the capital to the other, affecting every house, every factory, every hospital. Nobody is safe from the choking red gunk, and nobody seems to know where it has come from.

Something is rotten under London.

I go to my school bag, where I dumped it not ten

minutes before. In those ten minutes, everything has changed. To think I had considered – even for a moment – giving up being a detective! I take out my notebook and flip it open. I turn to a new page and write . . .

LONDON IS POISONED.

🔑

Night has fallen and I'm in my room, sitting on the bed with the skylight open. I'm mending the rip in my school skirt by torchlight while listening to the radio. I'm supposed to be asleep, so the volume is turned right down, the speaker close to my ear. Every couple of minutes I change station, but they're all saying the same thing.

'Red algae have spread through . . .'

'The water supply of London has been infected by . . .'

'The slime, described by Richard in Islington as "like something out of a horror movie" . . .'

I listen to it all. When the skirt is mended, I set it to one side and look up through the skylight to the hazy stars. On the breeze I can hear sirens, ringing around London like a headache. Every so often a helicopter passes, but whether they're police or television crews, filming the city from above, I can't tell. All around me, London is in crisis.

And me?

I'm grounded.

As I lie perfectly still, there is a battle raging in my head. On one hand, I'm terrified by the threat – the threat that someone will come for Dad. On the other hand (I'm not too proud to admit it) I'm excited! The incident with Professor D'Oliveira is a real case, a big case – why else would someone threaten me? I remember the sheet of newspaper that I had found on the professor. I take it out and unfold it. There is a small story – barely two paragraphs – about London water pollution.

> . . . Scientists confirmed today that the quality of London's water had declined in the last week, but refused to speculate about the origin of the pollution. While current levels of pollution are not dangerous for human consumption . . .

Well, it's definitely dangerous for human consumption now. And this story was written yesterday – before the crisis hit. Had Professor D'Oliveira known something about this beforehand? Now there was talk of quarantining London to stop the algae from spreading to the rest of the country, even the rest of the *world*.

I have my notebook in my hand, and I flip back between the two pages I'd written on that day – HIT-AND-RUN and LONDON POISONED. The more I think about it, the more I feel the two have to be connected. I can't see how yet; it's just an intuition, a hunch. I put the notebook down, but the words are still there, flashing in the stars above my skylight, back and forth until they get jumbled up –

HIT-AND-RUN

LONDON POISONED

HIT-AND-RUN

LONDON POISONED

So could the hit-and-run have something to do with the crisis? I take out the professor's card and read it again. Then I take down my dictionary and look up 'hydrology' – *The branch of science concerned with the properties of the earth's water.*

Finally, I take out my pen and write –

The polluted water seems to be coming from underground, not from the reservoirs north of London. Who would know more about the workings of underground London than a professor from the Royal Geographical Society, who specialises in hydrology, the study of water?

It's a flimsy connection, I have to admit – but doesn't Poirot often act on a suspicion, a hunch, an unproven fancy? I need to know more.

And there is my dilemma. If I want to know more,

I'll have to talk to Professor D'Oliveira, and in order to do that I'll have to leave the house. I'd be disobeying not just Dad, but the man who had attacked me as well. I can't be sure that he will go through with his threat, but I also can't assume that he won't. I lie here while all this is going through my mind, until a voice on the radio catches my attention. It's a reporter, just out of a conference held by the Metropolitan Police.

'At the moment, there seems little hope that the situation can be easily resolved. Fresh water – the lifeblood of the city – has stopped pumping around London. The heart of the capital has stopped, and this crisis will continue until someone finds a way to restart it.' He takes a breath, and even with the volume down I can hear how shaky he sounds. 'Right now, London needs a miracle.'

Poirot is sitting in a chair on the other side of the room in near darkness. His green eyes are shining like a cat's.

'London needs a miracle,' he repeats, tutting softly. '*Mon dieu.*'

'I could get into trouble,' I say to him.

'Ah, Mademoiselle Oddlow – trouble is all around. But heroes are rare.'

I turn off the radio and get out of bed. It's no good waiting for a miracle – somebody needs to act.

'Thanks, Hercule.'

He rises from his chair and bows goodbye. 'It is my pleasure.'

⚷

Someone might be watching me leaving the house, so I need a disguise. Thankfully, I've spent plenty of time preparing for this. I look through my wardrobe for a minute before settling on my outfit of choice – a white T-shirt, lace-up shoes and baby-blue medical scrubs. If I'm going to the hospital, I might as well look like a nurse.

The scrubs are loose fitting – nice in the hot weather, but I know I can't go out like this – I put on a knee-length navy trench coat and a matching floppy hat. I look in the mirror, checking everything over, then decide that my hair is too recognisable.

I replace the hat with a wig of honey-blonde hair and look again. Now I doubt even Dad would recognise me in the street. I'm roasting, though.

Disguise complete, I step up on the bed and hoist myself out of the skylight. I sit on the roof for a moment. There's a breeze, but it's still warm. When I'm ready, I shuffle forward, down the slope of the roof, until I come to the edge. There's a rustle as my feet brush the leaves of the oak tree below. Putting one leg over, I feel around for the right branch.

I find my foothold and – with a deep breath – push into space.

The craggy tree is there to meet me, and I grip on to the trunk until I find my bearings. I start to climb down, finding old footholds, trying to be quiet. By the bottom, I've turned a half spiral round the tree, so its trunk is between me and the house. I peer round and can see the kitchen light on. Dad is hunched over the table, talking on the telephone. Before he can turn and see me, I steal across the garden lawn and out through the back gate.

Hyde Park is dark. I move quickly, jumping at

every rustle, every shadow. Before I reach the gates, a fox leaps out in front of me and I almost cry out. It scampers off, and I take a moment to compose myself. In another minute I come to the north edge of the park. The traffic ahead reassures me – when there are other people around I'm less scared that someone will drag me into the shadows.

I come out opposite Lancaster Gate underground station. My mobile is back in my room, so I cross the road and go into a telephone box outside the station. It smells dreadful inside, but it's worth it to remain anonymous. Someone might be tapping my phone.

Because Professor D'Oliveira was knocked down in Hyde Park, I know which hospital they will have taken her to – St Mary's, just a five-minute walk north of the park. I had my appendix taken out in the very same hospital, so I know it well. I wipe down the plastic receiver with my handkerchief and put a handful of change into the slot. Quickly, I Change Channel. A filing cabinet with handwritten cards appears in front of me, and I flip through to 'H' for hospital . . .

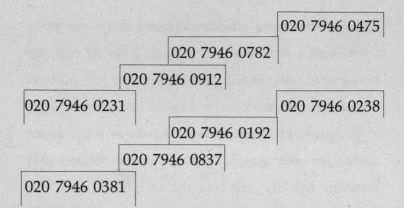

020 7946 0475

020 7946 0782

020 7946 0912

020 7946 0231   020 7946 0238

020 7946 0192

020 7946 0837

020 7946 0381

Ah! There we go – I dial the hospital reception's number from memory.

'St Mary's Hospital, how can I help?' a chirpy voice says.

'Ah yes, 'ello,' I say, adopting a French accent and lowering my voice an octave, 'I am telephoning you to enquire about – 'ow you say? – my aunt. I sink she was taken to your 'ospital earlier today.'

'Name?'

'My name? It iz . . .'

'No, not your name – hers.'

'Ah, *mais oui*! Dorothée D'Oliveira.'

'Hang on a second.'

I listen to her typing on a keyboard, while I

worry that my handful of change will run out.

'Hello? Yes, she's staying the night for observation, but visiting hours are over – you'll have to come tomorrow.'

The phone starts to beep – I'm about to be cut off.

'Ah, but of course! Could I have ze details of ze ward?'

She tells me the wing and ward in which the professor is staying, and the hours I can visit her the next day.

'Ah, sank you, *merci*!'

The phone goes dead, and my change clunks into the belly of the machine.

'Good work, Agatha,' I say to myself. 'Now you just need to break into a hospital without getting arrested.'

St Mary's is as busy as ever – ambulances coming and going, people smoking and talking outside the main gates. I notice a number of tankers, parked in a line down Praed Street, in front of the main building. I guess they're delivering fresh water – nowhere in the city will be worse affected by the crisis than hospitals.

I know if I go in through the main entrance I'll be spotted. I walk to the end of the street and turn down South Wharf Road – the back of the hospital buildings. Keeping my head down, I walk until halfway down the road I come to an open bay door, next to which is parked one of the huge trucks. A thick plastic pipe runs from the tanker into the dimly lit bay. There is a whooshing, gurgling noise as the water is drained.

I stop and pretend to search for a phone in my pocket. Carrying a mobile gives you an excuse to stop dead in the street and look gormless. The only person I can see who's watching over things is the lorry driver, leaning against the wall by the bay, smoking a cigarette. He isn't watching the lorry, but something inside the bay – a pressure gauge, perhaps. He isn't wearing his security pass, which is resting on a piece of machinery next to him.

I stand for a second, weighing up my options. I look at the lorry and at the street. Then, before I draw attention to myself by standing there too long, I cross the road and walk until the lorry is between me and the driver. Stepping up on the metal plate, I reach for the handle, hoping he has left his door locked. He has – the handle doesn't give. I yank it a couple more times, but nothing happens. Exasperated, I draw my foot back and give the truck a hard kick.

'Ow ow ow!' I mutter under my breath, toes smarting.

Nothing happens for a second.

The truck's alarm goes off, scaring me half to death. Quickly, I jump down from the plate and walk round to the other side of the lorry where the driver is still smoking his cigarette. He's frowning, looking at his truck with its alarm blaring and lights flashing, when I go up to him.

"Scuse me, mister, some kid's trying to break into your truck!' I say.

'What . . .' he begins, then swears loudly and runs round the side. Quickly, I duck inside the bay, past an array of pipes and gauges to a door at the back. I grab his security pass as I go and press it to the door release. It beeps once and the door opens. I breathe a sigh of relief and step through.

I inspect my outfit – immaculate – before hurrying

down the corridor, away from the angry shouts of the truck driver, who must have returned to his station to find the pass missing. I take off my coat and stash it in an alcove. I fix my blonde wig back with a scrunchie and a couple of hair slides.

Showtime.

I spend the next quarter of an hour navigating my way through the service corridors of the hospital, many of them quiet and unlit, listening for sounds of activity. The hallways go from bare brick with pipes and cables to old, chipped plaster, full of cleaning supplies and mop buckets. Finally, fresh-painted walls – corridors through which doctors, nurses and porters can move quickly around the hospital.

After a close call with a woman collecting laundry, and another with a porter wheeling a patient on a trolley, I make my way to the professor's ward. Several people see me, but none of them close up. From a distance, I can pass for one of the nursing staff.

Entering through the caretaker's door, I avoid going past the ward reception. At the other end of the ward I can see a nurse sitting at her station, reading. Everything else is dark – closed doors on either side. Some have dim lights behind their misted glass – reading lamps or televisions. I wonder if patients are staying up to watch the news of London's crisis.

Starting to move down the ward, I peer in the half light at each door, on which is a whiteboard giving the names of the patients. The rooms have up to four people in them, but when I find the professor's room, halfway down the ward, her name is alone on the board. Through the misted glass, I can see that the lights are off. I'd hoped she'd be awake to see me, but I haven't come this far to give up.

I try the handle. It's locked, but I know that hospital doors never have proper locks – they can always be opened easily from the outside, in case there's a medical emergency. Examining the handle, I see a turning piece with a groove down the centre. I used all my spare change back at the telephone box, but I take one of the clips from my hair, fit it into the groove, and turn the mechanism. The door clicks.

Not wanting to alert the night nurse to my presence, I step inside the room before saying anything, and close the door behind me.

'Hello—' is all I manage, before something hard whistles through the darkness and cracks on the back of my head.

I tumble forward on to the floor, clutching my head.

Suddenly the lights are on.

'Who the hell are you?' A voice speaks above me. Not a male voice, nor a young one – it is an older woman's voice, with a hint of the Caribbean – Jamaica, at a guess, or possibly Trinidad. Slowly, half blinded by the light, I open my eyes and look up. Standing above me, with one arm in a sling and the other holding a metal crutch over her head, is Professor D'Oliveira. She looks more formidable than when she was unconscious.

'My name is Agatha.' I wince, keeping my arms over my head until she lowers the crutch.

'Who sent you?' Her gaze is piercing and I have trouble meeting it.

I push myself up to sitting, rubbing my head. The blow has left my blonde wig askew, and I remove it.

'Nobody sent me. I'm the one who found you in the park this morning.' I get to my feet with as much dignity as I can muster. My head is beginning to throb – she has quite a whack for an elderly woman.

'You called the ambulance?'

'Yes.'

She sighs and walks back to her bed, sits down and watches me. I wait for an apology, but none comes. There is a file full of papers next to her on the bed, which she reaches out and closes before I can see any of them.

'So, Agatha, what brings you to St Mary's in the middle of the night?'

I wrestle with my thoughts, trying not to give away my suspicions.

'I need to talk to you. Your card says you're a professor in hydrology?'

She raises an eyebrow.

'Not an ordinary schoolgirl, are we, Agatha?'

'I should hope not,' I say with some impatience.

She chuckles. She really is difficult to read.

'Ah, a bit of fire in the belly, I like that.' She studies me some more. 'Well, thank you, Agatha – you did me a good turn. Not all thirteen-year-olds would have stopped to help an old lady.'

'How do you know my age?'

She shrugs. 'A lucky guess.'

I let it pass. 'I was wondering – do you have any idea why someone would want to do that to you? Knock you over?'

I watch her face carefully as I say this, but her expression doesn't change.

'Oh –' she waves her hand airily – 'I'm sure it would be the same if some other little old lady had been standing in my place. Just a hooligan.'

Her tone is convincing, but I don't believe for one moment that she thinks of herself as a 'little old lady'.

'Well, did you see anything that might identify them?'

'No. And right now, I'm scarcely angrier with *them* than I am with *you*.'

I stare at her. 'Why?'

'I've had a nasty shock and I need to sleep, girl – not to be scared out of my wits by some picklock sneaking into my room in the dead of night. Now, please get out and leave me alone.'

She climbs into bed and puts her head on the pillow. Clearly, she feels the interview is over. I persevere –

'No close-up details of the bike perhaps, or what the rider was wearing? It went too quickly for me to get a good look.' This isn't entirely true – I could pick that bike out of a line-up – but I need to get her to open up.

She groans. 'I don't remember a thing. And if I did, I would be telling it to the police, not a schoolgirl.' She reaches up to the panel behind the bed, full of dials and buttons. 'And if you don't leave now, I'll press the emergency call button, and you can explain to the night guard why you're creeping around the hospital in the dark, scaring old ladies.'

'But—'

I don't finish: she presses the emergency call button, and a red light starts to flash over the door.

Outside, I can hear an alarm ringing at the nurses' station.

Wasting no time, I make for the door. But, as I do, something catches my attention – a pair of shoes – Professor D'Oliveira's shoes – left next to the door. On the side of one of the shoes . . . is that a trace of red? I have no more time to think about it – I have to keep moving, out of the room.

'Hey, stop! Who are you? You're not allowed in there!' a nurse calls to my fast-retreating back. I ignore her and run out of the ward, back into the maze of corridors. I sprint down two flights of stairs and into another hospital block, retracing my path from earlier. When I'm sure nobody is trying to chase me, I slow down. I listen round every corner in case someone is there. The more I listen, the more I feel like I'm being watched. The dark corridors echo, and every so often I can hear linoleum squeaking with footsteps.

Finally, I come back to the corridor where I stashed my things. I put my coat on quickly and keep walking. I'd left the wig behind, so my disguise is a bit lacking now. I walk out into another bay at the back of the hospital, where surgical supplies are being unloaded.

'Hey, kid! You're not meant to be back here.'

'I'm leaving, aren't I?'

I walk out on to South Wharf Road. A girl is standing on the other side of the street, just quietly watching me. My heart thumps in shock. Forcing myself to react, I realise my only option is to turn back into the bay. But then the girl crosses the road towards me, and I see it's Brianna Pike, from school. I'm so relieved to see a familiar face that I almost throw my arms round her. Then I remember that she is one of the CCs, practically Sarah Rathbone's henchwoman. Brianna is tall and slim, like her compatriots, but more athletic – muscular.

She doesn't greet me, but asks 'How is she?' in a low voice.

'Who?' I don't think I've ever been asked a question by Brianna before. She's usually giving orders.

'The old lady.'

'You mean Professor D'Oliveira?'

'Is that her name?'

I sigh. 'How do you know about her? Brianna, what are you doing here?'

'I just . . . I heard about the old lady getting knocked down.'

I frown at her. 'How did you hear?' She's not acting like herself. If anything, it seems like someone else is standing in front of me, in a very convincing Brianna disguise.

'Oh . . . I read about it in the paper. I knew your dad worked at the park, so . . .' She tails off.

None of it adds up. I'm sure there was no report in the paper, and why would Brianna care anyway? All that interests her are designer outfits.

There's a long silence.

'Look,' I say at last, 'I really need to get home . . .'

She jolts, as though she'd forgotten where she is – or who I am. 'Sure, sure. I'll see you at school . . . My brother's got the car round the corner. Do you want a lift?'

I'm tempted by the thought of not having to walk back home in the dark, but I'm not ready to get in a car with one of the CCs. I shake my head.

'No, it's OK, thanks – it's not far. See you then, Brianna.' I walk away, mulling over the weird conversation.

London is still too quiet. Even at night, the city usually has a low hum, like a machine on standby.

I turn a corner and keep walking. There's the roar of a motorbike behind me on the otherwise empty road. My skin prickles. Keeping my head down I slow my pace, as though I'm just out for a stroll, enjoying the night air. The bike comes nearer. It's the same bike from earlier in the park – the one whose rider Dad argued with; the one that knocked down the professor. I'm sure of it.

Riding the bike is a man dressed all in black. I hold my breath, waiting for him to pass. He seems to slow down, then turns his head and looks right at me as he passes. I see myself, reflected in the mirrored visor. Then, with a grunt from the engine that makes my stomach twist, the bike speeds off.

'Oh, no.' I say, 'No, no, no . . .'

I start to run. Did they recognise me? Has the professor called someone? Is she in cahoots with the man on the bike? I have no idea, but I need to get home to Dad before the man on the bike beats me to it. My feet pound the pavement, past Paddington Station, through Sussex Gardens, across Bayswater Road, until the familiar park surrounds me – the park that now seems like a trap. I run, even though my legs are burning and I feel sick and heavy-headed.

Finally, I'm home – the back garden and the tree. I climb without care, branches scraping my arms and face, in through the skylight. Quickly, making no noise, I go down the attic stairs to Dad's bedroom. Tiptoeing over, I open the door and hear his familiar, gentle snores.

All at once the fear bleeds out of me and I sink to the floor. I listen as my heartbeat slows and the pain in my legs fades.

Twenty minutes pass.

At last I'm calm.

Calm, and very tired. Nobody seems to be coming to the house – not tonight anyway – but I can't bring myself to sleep upstairs. I go to my room, get changed, and put away my coat and scrubs. Then I fetch my duvet and pillows, make a nest for myself next to Dad's bedroom door, and sleep.

6.

THE MiSSiNG PLANS

I had hoped to wake before Dad, but he's up first, and nudges me awake with his slipper.

'Agatha? What are you doing on the floor?'

'I . . . had a bad dream.'

He smiles and frowns at the same time.

'That bad, huh?'

'Pretty bad.' I get up and hug him. 'Want coffee?'

'Please. Big day ahead.' He sighs, remembering everything that has happened the day before. 'I feel like I had a bad dream too.'

'Maybe I can help out in the park today,' I say. 'I bet St Regis will be closed without water . . .'

He chuckles at my optimism. 'Nice try. I've been listening to the radio – sounds like everywhere *but* St Regis is closed. They've shipped in water especially for you.'

I groan.

Dad is right – St Regis is open for business. Lesser schools might have been closed down by the 'minor crisis', but St Regis – the school of choice for the sons and daughters of billionaires and oligarchs – is not going to be brought down by something as trifling as a water shortage. So, I will have to sit through maths and chemistry, wishing I could be investigating, but most of all wishing I could keep an eye on Dad.

My first lesson is dance in the Great Hall. Liam must have arrived a little while before me because he's already changed and standing in the corridor outside the hall. I see Brianna Pike nearby, but the other CCs are standing apart from her. Sarah and Ruth talk to each other closely, as though sharing a secret. This is nothing new. They like to make everyone else feel like they aren't in on the joke.

Quickly, I change into my dress and shoes and

join the class. We all hate ballroom dancing, but there's some generous donor on the board of governors who thinks all young ladies and gentlemen need to learn, so we have no choice. I can't wait to tell Liam about everything that happened yesterday and luckily, as we are partners, I don't have long to wait. Liam and I were paired together at the start of term. Unluckily, we are both *dreadful*. The portraits of St Regis' past alumni look disdainfully down on us – surely all of them knew how to dance a foxtrot.

Liam shuffles over quickly, dying to talk.

'Agatha, have you seen the news?'

'Of course I have – and I do have so much more to tell you,' I say in a low voice. But, just as I'm about to recount my tale, the music starts. As Liam stands on my foot during the warm-up and mumbles an apology, I lean in to his ear, 'I think the water crisis is linked to the hit-and-run.'

'Whaaat?' He looks sharply at me. 'How can it be?'

'Because Dorothy D'Oliveira is a professor of

hydrol— OW! –' Liam has trodden on my foot again – 'Careful!'

'Sorry, sorry . . . Howz about you explain everything and I'll concentrate on not stepping on your toes?'

So I do, telling Liam about everything that happened since I'd left him at school yesterday. I tell him about the assault outside the RGS, the mysterious biker, my encounter with Professor D'Oliveira and Brianna Pike. For a moment, I'm aware of Brianna and her partner dancing closely to us, in perfect time, but then they're gone. She's with a tall, dark-haired boy who's rumoured to be from the dethroned royal family of a small country in Eastern Europe. Fleetingly, I wonder if Brianna has heard any of my story.

I finish up – 'And I could have *sworn* that I saw the red slime on her shoe as I left . . . It can't just be a coincidence. The professor went to hospital early in the day – before the first sightings of the slime!'

Liam doesn't say anything for a long moment, but I can't be sure if he's thinking about what I'd said, or concentrating on not tripping up. Our steps are even more out of step than usual. Finally, he says –

'Look, Agatha, don't you think this investigation is a bit . . . over our heads?'

'Liam, this is the best case we've ever had!' I cry out. 'I need your help more than ever. I need *you*, Liam.'

'Ahem! You do realise the music has stopped, Miss Oddlow, Mr Lau?' The teacher's voice makes us spring apart.

The others in the class are sniggering, and I blush in spite of myself.

'Nice one, Oddball.' Sarah Rathbone grins. Next is the polka – a particularly evil dance, which never seems to fit the music. With the music back to cover our voices, I do my best to convince Liam.

'London needs us – this is a real crisis, not a missing cat.'

Turn, sidestep, hop, reverse.

'I don't know . . . Shouldn't we leave it to the police?'

'But they don't have the leads that we have,' I say.

'Change partners! Keep your back straight, Mr Fitzpatrick. Tem-po!' the teacher interrupts our conversation.

Liam spins away from me, into the arms of another girl, and by the time he returns he seems to have made up his mind. 'Agatha, look, you're my best friend . . . If this case is so important to you, then count me in. Just try not to get us locked up because of it.' He grins, and my heart leaps.

'Thanks, Liam, that really means— ouch!'

'Sorry.'

'Mr Lau, could you at least attempt to hear the hop in the music?' calls the teacher.

Liam smiles and whispers into my ear, 'Apparently, there's a hop in the music.'

I shake my head, smiling. With Liam on board it really is going to be a proper investigation.

After the lesson, I put my regular shoes back on, rubbing my bruised toes, and go to the toilets to splash water on my face. My hair is a mess from all the whirling around. I look at my flushed cheeks, then stand in front of the mirror and run a brush through my dark bob. I think I'm alone, until I hear a whimper from one of the cubicles. I jump at the unexpected sound – yesterday wasn't good for my nerves. I pull myself together.

'Hello?'

There's no reply except for a choked sob.

'Hello?' I repeat, going over to the cubicle and tapping the door. 'Are you OK in there?'

There's no sound for a second, then the door unlocks.

'Come in,' says a voice. I know that voice, and for a moment I hesitate – surely this is a set-up? But, for whatever reason, I do as she says.

Brianna Pike is sitting inside, muddy tracks of mascara streaking her cheeks. I'm so used to Brianna wearing a certain expression – haughty disdain – that it takes me a moment to realise she's crying.

'Brianna . . . what's the matter?'

'Lock the door. I don't want anyone coming in . . . Please?'

I hesitate, then do as she says. It's pretty cramped in here. 'What's happened?'

She doesn't say anything, just shows me the screen of her smart phone. I look at it, trying to understand. I rarely use social media, but I grasp a few key facts –

1. *There is a photo of Brianna's face.*
2. *Unlike the many photos of Brianna's face (posted by Brianna), this has been posted by someone else.*
3. *That someone else is Sarah Rathbone.*
4. *The photo is NOT flattering.*

'Sarah posted that?' I ask carefully.

'Yes . . . And the caption is "Hot or Not?"' The words bring Brianna to another spasm of tears. Her shoulders shake and her make-up dissolves further.

'I take it the comments weren't . . . positive?'

She shakes her head. 'She took that picture before I'd put my make-up on after a sleepover and I'd hardly had any sleep and . . .'

Now I fully understand what has happened, but I feel like I understand nothing. Who cares about a spot of make-up? Still, I try to be sensitive to Brianna's tears. 'But . . . why would she do that?' I ask. 'I thought you were friends?'

Brianna tears off some toilet paper and dries her eyes. 'Me too –' she sighs – 'but I guess she wanted to show me who's boss . . . That we're friends because she *lets* us be friends.'

I shake my head. 'That doesn't sound like much of a friendship. Why do you hang out with her?'

Brianna shrugs, but doesn't say anything. Her tears seemed genuine, but I feel uneasy – Brianna has been as mean to me as Sarah and Ruth since my first day at St Regis. What's changed now? Everything seems too convenient, too much like a trap. Everywhere I go, she turns up and with what's going on in London, I don't know who I really can trust.

'Brianna, I have to ask – what were you doing outside the hospital last night?'

Brianna stops drying her eyes and looks right at me. She seems to have forgotten the photo, forgotten Sarah's betrayal. For a moment, she looks defensive, her old, cocky self. Then she looks away.

'I . . . I can't tell you here.'

'What?'

'I can't tell you . . . someone might overhear. Come to my house . . . tonight.'

We leave the cubicle. She takes a piece of paper

from her school bag and writes a mobile number and an address. 'If you come, I'll tell you.'

She hands the piece of paper to me and goes quickly, leaving me dazed and confused in the girls' lavatories.

Finally, after the slowest Friday on record, the bell rings, and we almost run out of the gates. I need to do some urgent research into London's water supply. With Liam at my side I flag down a black cab.

'St James's Square, please.'

St James's Square is home to the London Library – my favourite place in the whole world. I have a young person's membership, which I begged Dad to buy me as a combined birthday and Christmas present. The library is full of rare books, manuscripts and old newspapers. Agatha Christie used to be a member, and sometimes I pause and wonder, romantically, if I'm reading the same monograph on blood-spatter patterns that she did all those years ago.

But this is no time to be whimsical – something nasty is going on! If this isn't an opportunity for greatness, stretching its hand out to mine, I don't know what is. We spend the taxi ride talking about what we need to search for. Part of my mind is still on Brianna, and what happened in the toilets.

'Liam, can I borrow your phone for a minute?'

'Sure – what are you looking for?'

'Oh, just something to do with the algae,' I lie, taking it from him. Quickly, I search for Brianna's social media account, where she posts all her photos. It's all there for anyone to see – countless pictures of Brianna smiling, pouting, posing. She's wearing all sorts of designer outfits, standing in front of palm trees or next to swimming pools. I scroll through them all, trying to decide if I'm imagining the hollow look in her eyes.

'Find what you're looking for?' Liam asks, frowning a little.

'Oh, uh, no . . .' I say, closing the page and handing the phone back.

I'm not ready to tell Liam about what happened with Brianna, or her promise to tell me more. I don't know what I think about any of it. I think he would

114

tell me not to visit her at home, but I'm curious to hear her story.

The receptionist at the library recognises me.

'Afternoon, Miss Agatha.'

'Afternoon, Clive. This is Liam. Would it be all right for him to come in with me?'

'Well, I really shouldn't . . .' Clive starts. He taps his nose and winks. 'But so long as you don't tell anyone . . .'

'Thank you, Clive – I owe you one. Can we have a locker for our satchels?'

'Of course.'

He hands me a key, and presses the button to open the gate. We hurry in, place our things in the locker and practically run up the grand staircase. The portraits of the library's illustrious patrons look down on us. We pass Lord Tennyson, George Eliot, Charles Dickens, and, looking particularly disapproving outside the men's toilets, Winston Churchill.

We reach the second floor and go into the stacks where the books are stored. The stacks of the London Library are unlike any others – all the floors are made of cast iron, with slats for ventilation, so you can see several floors below and above you, and glimpse people passing underneath as they browse.

'Wow,' Liam says, looking up, then down. 'I feel a bit dizzy.'

'You'll get used to it. Come on, follow me.'

I move quickly, knowing already where I want to go. Halfway down the shelf of engineering periodicals, I find them – a dusty bundle of plans for the London water mains. As we browse, I can hear someone's footsteps echoing through the iron frame above us, coming closer. They seem to stop, right above us, and I look up. Strangely, the lights for the next level are switched off. Though they can see us, we can't see them.

'There's someone there,' Liam whispers, flicking his eyes up.

'I know,' I whisper back. 'Come on – these are all we need.'

We gather the plans and hurry to the Reading Room. If there's a crisis quietly spreading through the rest of London, you wouldn't know it here. It's quiet in the Reading Room, just like always. The leather armchairs are filled with ex-Oxford dons and retired politicians writing their memoirs. They're not disturbed by the rising red gunge around them, but the arrival of a couple of thirteen-year-old schoolkids is greeted with frowns and murmurs.

I sit down at one of the reading desks and lay the contents of the bundle out in front of us. Liam pulls up a chair next to me. There are more frowns as his chair legs scrape on the wooden floor. The first map I come to is an overview of the water supply for London, titled 'Location of Ring Main Shafts and Tunnels'. It shows a rough circle drawn around the city, north and south of the Thames.

I read the description of the supply pipe, called the Ring Main – a gigantic loop, eighty kilometres long, and two and a half metres in diameter, encircling all of London. Strung along the line are shafts connecting the pipe to the surface. This is where the problem must be – somehow the red slime has found its way into the Ring Main, pumping in an endless circuit around London like diseased blood around a body.

But where has it come from? And how can it be growing underground, without sunlight, in the deep tunnels?

'So *this* is where the slime is coming from then?' Liam says.

'I think so. But how is it getting into the pipes?' I say, before someone shushes me.

I rummage through the other papers, which are all plans for the shafts. There seems to be something missing. I check the index for what the bundle should contain, and tick off everything on the list except one – the schematics for the Brixton Pumping Station. I try to think of everything I know about Brixton. I know there's a hidden river there, covered over by London's expansion. Could that be important?

'Come on,' I tell Liam.

It's time to get home – Dad will be back soon, and I don't want to disappoint him like I did yesterday. We trudge back on foot, tired and thirsty in the heat. But I'm also feeling a buzz of adrenaline. I'm getting used to it, ever since the masked biker skidded past me. Neither of us say much – we're too wrapped up in our thoughts. All kinds of sirens are wailing in the streets around us – police, fire and ambulance. We pass two men yelling at each other in the middle of the road. The lack of water is making everyone crazy. Liam walks with me until he reaches his bus stop.

'Before I go – about the symbol you showed me yesterday, the tattoo?'

'Yes? Have you found something?' I perk up.

'No, the opposite – I looked at, like, *the whole internet*. Nothing. It looks like a key, but there are millions of pictures of keys out there. Are you sure you remembered it right?'

I shoot him a withering look – my memory is photographic.

'All right, hold your fire,' he says, pretending to hide from my dagger-eyes. 'Whatever it is, it's a mystery to me.'

'But that can't be right – I feel sure I've seen that symbol before. Can you check one more time?'

He grimaces. 'Urgh . . . all right.'

A bus pulls up.

'See you soon,' he says and waves, as he joins the queue to board.

I wave back, then walk the rest of the way to Hyde Park. Police cars and ambulances speed in opposite directions, but there are hardly any cars on the road – people aren't going out, aren't going to work. Offices have no water for making drinks, flushing toilets or washing hands. Without water, London is starting to grind to a halt.

It's almost five by the time I get in, and I'm tired. It's time, as Poirot would say, to sit back and use my 'little grey cells' to figure it out. Not wanting to waste time, I go straight upstairs, sit on my bed and close my eyes. Just a minute later, I hear the front door open, and the sound of Dad lugging something into the hallway.

The front door closes, and I wait, listening to the sounds from the kitchen – a lot of banging about. Usually, Dad will call up the stairs, but he seems to be busy with whatever he's doing. Feeling curious, I go to see what the commotion is. Peering round the doorframe, I see the worktop and kitchen table cluttered up.

'Hey, Dad?'

'Hmmf,' he says, gripping a length of rubber tubing in his mouth.

'What are you doing?' I ask. I'm not used to doing the questioning. On the worktop next to the sink, seven demijohn bottles are lined up. Dad usually uses them for making fruit wines from rosehips and wild plums he gathers in the park, but now they're full of the evil red slime. Each one is fitted with a valve to let air out but not in, and these are attached to rubber pipes that lead out of the window. Dad takes the tubing from his mouth.

'It's what you would call an experiment.'

'Are you still trying to kill the algae?' I frown, listening to the slow *bloop-bloop* sound of air bubbles passing through the valves.

'Nope, I've tried everything – even the weedkillers and chemicals I swore I'd never use.' He coughs drily and I'm worried about how long he's been spending breathing in weedkillers and toxic slime.

'But, if you can't kill them, what's all this for?'

He turns to look at me for the first time, eyes pink and watering. 'This stuff must be growing underground, right?'

'Right.'

'Well, how? It doesn't use sunlight to grow – so where does it get its energy from?'

'So you're . . . feeding it?'

'Exactly!'

He has a feverish look in his eyes – I've never seen him like this. Since Dad is usually so calm and quiet, I've always thought that I get my, ahem, *obsessive* nature from Mum. Seeing him here, taping up bits of pipe and painting each of the bottles black to keep the light out, I'm not so sure.

'This one, I'm going to feed with plant matter – vegetable peelings and the like. This one, with meat – I've put a cut-up pork chop in there . . .'

Dad is talking to himself as much as to me. I nod along reassuringly, as though he's telling me he is the reincarnation of Julius Caesar, or that the royal family are giant lizards, but he doesn't seem to notice.

Finally, I make my excuses and go back up to my room. Everything is crazy, and Dad is acting crazy, and I need to be alone for a bit or I think I'll go crazy too.

7.

BREAKING AND ENTERING

I sit in my room for a long time, waiting until Dad thinks I'm asleep. All the while, I'm thinking about my next move, Changing Channel over and over again, going back to the places I've been in the last forty-eight hours.

I'm in the hospital room, looking down at the professor's red-stained shoes . . .

I'm outside the RGS, with a rag clamped over my mouth . . .

I'm in the park, watching in slo-mo as the motorbike roars towards me . . .

Two things keep bothering me – the professor's

link to the crisis, and my conversation with Brianna in the toilets. Since the professor is unwilling to be questioned, I might as well go and see Brianna.

Brianna Pike – heir to the Pike rubber glove fortune – lives in a townhouse on Cadogan Place. Brianna never speaks about her father's rubber glove business of course – that would be too embarrassing for a pupil at St Regis. The house is known among the older students at St Regis as the 'Party Palace', though obviously I've never been invited. Her big brother – a former St Regis pupil – is famous for his lavish lifestyle.

When I'm sure Dad will believe I'm asleep, I get dressed again. I get into my cut-off denim shorts and put on a red stripey vest top and my favourite blue creeper shoes. I pin my hair up and add a short ginger wig for disguise. If the mysterious biker is still around, I'd rather not look like myself. I slip my notebook and pen into my pocket. Then I open the skylight, get up on my chair and climb on to the roof. I move to where the tree reaches its branch and start climbing down. At the bottom, I dust myself off and check for onlookers, before running out through the back gate and into the park.

I run as much of the way as I can, checking around me at every corner. I try not to allow my imagination to roam into the realms of fear – bogeymen are for children, I tell myself. The light is fading when I reach Brianna's house, but at this time of the year it never gets totally dark – even in the middle of the night the sun barely dips under the horizon. The sky is full of pink-and-gold clouds, and you could have been forgiven for thinking that all is well – that this is a peaceful midsummer's night.

In the pit of my belly there is a churning unease – a feeling that, at any moment, a figure might drag me into the shadows. On the other side of the square is the Cadogan Hotel, where Oscar Wilde was arrested and dragged off to prison. For all the grandeur of the buildings, this seems a gloomy, haunted part of the city.

I decide to watch the house for a few minutes before risking ringing the doorbell. I lean against the railings a little further down the street. The plants here are suffering from the water shortage. I take my notebook and pen from my pocket. A light comes on and off again in Brianna's house, but that's about it. If Brianna is up to anything shady, she's being discreet. A motorbike drives down the street and stops a few houses past Brianna's.

I freeze.

I watch as a man gets off the bike and walks up her steps. He's still wearing his helmet, and is carrying something in front of him that I can't see. I check my watch – gone ten o'clock. The man glances round, then tries the door handle. Finding it unlocked, he goes in.

I stand for a moment, unresolved. Something is wrong. My heart is beating so quickly as I start to walk towards the house. Then my brain catches up. I have to hurry – Brianna might be in danger. I run along the street, up to the door, which is still ajar. As I run, the man emerges at the door, sprints the short distance to the bike, and rides off quickly.

'Brianna?' I whisper.

I run up to the front door and try the handle, finding it still unlocked. I push the door back to reveal a checkerboard floor in black and white marble and a well-lit corridor. I step in and make my way down the hallway. Suddenly, I wish I'd told Liam where I'm going.

'Brianna?' I try again.

There is a tiny muffled sound. My heart is racing. I walk a little way further down the hall, to a door that is slightly ajar. There is a light on in the room. I fling the door open to reveal . . .

Brianna, looking like a startled deer, with a slice of pepperoni pizza in her mouth. She gulps the pizza down, not taking her eyes off me for a second.

'Agatha, is that you under that wig? What the heck? You scared the bejeezus out of me!'

'Oh, I'm . . .' I look round, as though the explanation is behind me somewhere. 'There was a man . . . he let himself in.'

Brianna sighs, though I can't tell if it's relief or anger. We're in a book-lined study, with leather armchairs and a huge fireplace. Brianna is sitting in a chair.

'That was the pizza guy.' She points to the open box on her lap. 'Who did you think it was? A trained assassin?'

'But he just let himself in!'

'Yeah, I always leave the door unlocked for him.'

'But anyone could just walk in here.'

She grins. 'And yet, you're the first person who actually has, Agatha.'

'You invited me, remember?'

'Well, thanks for coming.' She tucks her sleek hair behind one ear, trying to regain some lost dignity. Her composure is back. She wears the same, self-confident smile that she used to have. For a moment, I'm sure she's going to kick me out of her house, the same way she would kick me out of the classroom if the CCs wanted it to themselves.

'Mummy and Daddy are in Switzerland, but my brother should have been back by now – he must have met up with one of his girlfriends.'

'How many does he have?'

She shrugs. 'I've lost count. They all seem like the same person to me.'

Whereas you seem like several different people to me, I think to myself.

'Want a drink?' She walks to a colossal globe, which stands on one side of the fireplace, and pushes a hidden catch. The Northern Hemisphere swings up to reveal a cocktail cabinet.

'Not for me, thanks.'

She laughs. 'It's not alcohol, dummy! Look.' She holds up a bottle of elderflower cordial and pours a glass.

I decide to try the direct approach. 'What were you going to tell me?'

She stands still for a second, as if deliberating something. Then says, 'You like investigating, don't you, Agatha?'

The question isn't the usual accusation – that I'm a snooper, a nosy parker, so I nod. 'Yes.'

'Well . . . I've never told anyone this . . . but well, so do I.'

'You?' I splutter. 'YOU like investigating?'

'Does it seem so unbelievable?' She grins – an expression I've never seen on her face before. Then she looks bashful.

I don't know what to say. 'Well . . .'

'Come on, I'll show you.' She makes for the bookcase at the back of the study, still cradling the tumbler of elderflower. The shelves look like all the others with a light switch next to them. Brianna flips up the casing of the light switch to reveal a security keypad, into which she punches a number. The bookcase clicks and swings smoothly back to reveal a hidden room. She turns to look at me out of the corner of her eye, as if to say, 'Cool, huh?' but I don't comment.

I hesitate for a moment. Do I really want to go into a secret room with a girl I don't trust – a girl who I'm not sure I even really like?

'Come on,' she says. She catches my expression. 'I promise not to feed you to the alligators I keep in the basement.'

I can't help smiling at that, although nothing about this weird encounter would surprise me. I follow her through the door and she turns the lights on. The room is small, barely more than a cupboard, but it has a desk and lots of shelves. The shelves are crammed with technology – gadgets from microscopes to battery-powered drones. There's stuff that even I don't recognise.

'Wow,' I say. I've always thought that Brianna was more interested in impressing boys than anything else. I didn't expect her to have a secret lair. Well, not *this* kind of secret lair anyway. Perhaps something more with mood lighting and a minibar.

'Yeah, I kinda cleared out the spy gadget shop in Covent Garden.' She turns to me. 'So what do you think?'

I look around, trying to decide what I think.

'What are these?' I ask, pointing out what looks like the sort of thing a tree surgeon or gardener would wear to protect his eyes.

'They're night-vision goggles,' Brianna answers me.

'And this?'

'A long-range listening device. Cool, huh?'

I look sideways at Brianna. Am I hearing things right?

'And is that *actual* luminol?' I ask, pointing to a

spray bottle. Police use luminol to detect where blood has been cleaned up in a room – it glows bright blue where the blood had been, revealing the gruesome spatters. I've wanted to get my hands on some for ages.

'Sure.' Brianna grins lopsidedly. 'Ooh, and check out this robotic camera!' She holds it out proudly.

'This is all amazing.' I choose my words carefully.

'Thanks,' she says, clearly aware of what I'm not saying, 'but I know what you're thinking.'

'You do?'

'You're wondering why I have all this stuff when at school I'm such an airhead.'

'I guess, yeah.' I look around the room. 'I can't quite believe this is *you*, Brianna.'

She nods sadly – I'm confirming what she already knows.

'I'm not like you, Agatha. I care what other people think.'

'Well, you're more like me than I'd ever have guessed,' I say hesitantly.

'That's not what I mean.' Brianna shrugs. 'You're

so . . . good at being yourself. You don't seem to care if people like you or not, but I'm not like that, Agatha. I just want to fit in . . . I've never even used any of this stuff before.'

'What, you've never tried it out?'

'Only at home – not to actually solve a crime or catch a criminal. I've never had a real adventure.'

She says the word 'adventure' with a kind of longing that I know only too well. Suddenly I like Brianna Pike a whole lot more than I thought.

'Fitting in is one thing.' I incline my head. 'It doesn't mean you have to turn yourself into a *Carbon Copy*.' I catch my tongue, realising I've used the secret name for the CCs. For a moment, I'm scared of her reaction. Then Brianna laughs.

'Is that what people call us? It's pretty good, actually.'

I breathe a sigh of relief.

'They're not so bad, you know, Sarah and Ruth,' she says slowly, as though not quite believing her own words. 'They just wouldn't understand any of this.'

'Well, I know this won't change anything at

school,' I say, 'but it's good to know that there's a like mind at St Regis.'

She shrugs the compliment off. I'm prepared to like her, but there's still one question that I need an answer to.

'Brianna – what were you doing outside the hospital last night?'

She looks guilty.

'Honestly? You really want to know? I, uh . . . I was following you.'

'Following *me*?' And there I was thinking she might have had something more to do with it than I'd thought.

Brianna holds up her hands defensively. 'Yeah, but not, like, in a bad way! It's just . . . well, I heard you talking to Liam in class about what happened in the park, to that old lady . . .'

I nodded. 'I guessed you must have heard that.'

'And I dunno, I just felt like you were on to something – it seemed suspicious.'

I sigh. 'So why didn't you just say something?'

'Because . . .' She starts, then shrugs and suddenly

I understand – it wouldn't be easy for one of the CCs to ask to join Agatha Oddlow's geeky detective agency.

'Oh, I don't know,' she says. 'Can you forgive me?' She holds her hand out awkwardly. After a second I take it.

'Forgiven. Just stay away from my house with those night-vision goggles, OK?'

'You have my promise.' She laughs, crossing her heart. In spite of everything, I have to say that I trust her.

'Well.' I head towards the door. 'I'd better get home then, before my dad realises I'm gone.'

'I'll get you a cab.'

A cab?

Brianna not only calls a cab, she pays the driver in advance, refusing to listen to my objections.

'Drive safely,' she tells him.

'Will you be OK?' I ask her, remembering what had been going on between her and Sarah Rathbone.

'Me?' She tosses her blonde hair back with customary confidence. 'I'll be fine. Stay safe.'

'Stay safe, yourself.'

Grinning, she waves from the pavement as the taxi driver speeds off.

I sit in the back of the cab, mulling over the night's events. My visit has raised far more questions than it answered, but I'm also grinning as I cross the lawns. I might just be one step closer to having another friend.

As I get close to the house, I see a small yellow ribbon sticking out of a brick in the wall – Liam and my sign to each other.

'Yes!' I mutter under my breath. I crouch down and pull – the mortar there has come loose, and the brick comes away in my hand. In the darkness, you can't see anything in the hole, but when I pull the ribbon, there's a folded piece of paper attached. We came up with this hiding place for Liam to leave messages for me if I'm not at home and I have my phone switched off, as I usually do. I'm certain that the message must be something to do with Professor D'Oliveira's tattoo. I could read the message here, but I don't want to be seen and give away the location of our hiding place. So, I tuck the message into my pocket and replace the brick.

Back in my room, I take Liam's folded message out of my pocket and read –

Dear Aggie,

Just finished searching for the tattoo symbol AGAIN. My eyes are going square. Have triple-checked everything. May have found a lead, but will need more time to look into it.

Let me know if you have any more clues!

Liam

I shake my head, not understanding why the symbol might be so hard for Liam to find. I feel sure I've seen it before – I felt it the moment I spotted it on the professor's wrist. I search my memory, usually so reliable, but it's like grasping in the dark – one minute I'm groping around and think I have something, and the next it's gone in a whisper.

I change into my pyjamas, lie down on the bed on top of my duvet, and try to cool myself using a paper fan. I should be exhausted. Instead, I'm buzzing with thoughts – the little grey cells are hard at work, but making little progress.

I stare up at the deep-pink night clouds through my skylight and go over everything that has happened in the past couple of days. I've gone from Agatha the Invisible to somebody worth threatening. That means I've become a menace to someone in my own right. But who? Part of me relishes the idea that there is someone – perhaps more than one person – who believes I have the power to make a difference, to foil their plot or blow their cover, and part of me is just a little scared.

Quickly, I write out the facts across two pages of my notebook, drawing arrows where I suspect events are linked. There's the red slime, my assailant outside the RGS. Then there's Professor D'Oliveira – an old woman with a strange tattoo – and her hit-and-run ...

Suddenly I jump, as a knock sounds on the front door downstairs. I glance at the clock; it's almost eleven at night. Who would come this late? I hear Dad open the door and greet the visitor. So he must have been expecting them. I peer out from between my curtains, but catch only a glimpse of the person's head as they walk in. I feel nervous. After my attack outside the RGS, I'm wary about anyone visiting Dad – how do I know they are who they say they are?

I wait until I hear the door close and two pairs of feet make their way along the hall to the kitchen. Then I pull on my slippers to muffle my footsteps and creep downstairs. Oliver runs to me with a loud mewl halfway down. I freeze, convinced he has blown my cover. But there's no break in the conversation drifting up from downstairs. The staircase is enclosed, with a wall either side, and a door at the bottom that leads out to the hall. I open this door slightly, so I can eavesdrop, then scoop Oliver up.

We sit together, near the foot of the stairs, me trying to hear the conversation above Oliver's loud purring as he slumps in feline bliss on my lap.

I can only make out one side of the conversation. Dad's voice is soft and doesn't carry as well as the stranger's, which is loud and booming. It's a voice that is used to being listened to. There's no doubt that they're discussing the algae – the man's speech is punctuated with words like 'regeneration', 'abnormal growth rate' and 'unstable gas build-up'.

Despite his apparent knowledge, he sounds like a man who works in the City, buying and selling shares, rather than a research scientist. Research scientists tend to be quiet types, with a distracted air, but this man has a confidence that makes me sure, without seeing him, that he is dressed in a sharp suit.

I hear Dad say, 'So what's the verdict? How do we beat it, Mr, er . . . Davenport?'

'Well, I think you have the right idea with your lab, Rufe!'

'Nobody calls Dad "Rufe",' I whisper to Oliver. He stands on my lap and blows his salmony breath into my face, kneading my thighs with his sharp claws.

The man, Davenport, goes on – 'I'm sure you'll

get somewhere if you keep selectively starving the samples.'

'It would help if I knew what to starve them of,' Dad points out.

Davenport laughs. 'Good point, old boy, good point!'

I want to go and get a better look at this man. But, as I start to move, I hear Dad and the visitor come back out into the hall. I freeze on the bottom step, holding my breath and hope they won't spot me through the crack in the door.

I breathe out as Dad's voice sounds out at the front door, saying goodbye. Before he shuts the door, I hear him call out a greeting to JP and JP says hello in return. What is he doing outside our house so late at night, instead of sitting safely under the weeping tree?

My brain is racing. Images flash through my head as I try to process all the information. I'm suspecting everyone around me. The key's outline keeps coming back to me – the key tattoo on the professor's arm. There's something about that key . . . If I could only just remember . . . As I stand there deep in thought, I hear Dad turn the key in the front door, and know I need to move.

Oliver has given up hope of using me as his armchair, and is curled up on the landing.

I bend down to stroke him and an image flashes into my head.

It's just a snapshot, but I feel sure I've touched on it.

Quickly, I think hard so that the image is beamed on to the landing wall by an old-fashioned film projector. A key sketched in pencil I press the rewind lever on the projector. With a click and a whirr, the film reels backwards. Images dance on the wall, too fast to see. I press the forward lever and the film plays again – a hand reaching up to a bookshelf my own hand

Suddenly, the film jams in the projector and, a second later, catches fire against the hot bulb. There is no more – the memory is gone.

But it doesn't matter – I know where I need to look.

I run up the stairs and go to the bookcase in my

room. I scan the titles. There it is – an old copy of Agatha Christie's *Mysterious Affair at Styles*. Mum's book. I draw the novel from the shelf with shaking hands, and open the back cover. There it is – on the discoloured end page, a small sketch of the key. It's a perfect match with the professor's tattoo. Below the drawing of the key is a string of rough lines that look, at first glance, like something written in Viking runes . . .

IVIVXIIVIIIXIIIVIIIXIIVII

I'm breathless. Whatever is going on, Mum must have been involved, and she has left a message for me to find. I have seen this code in the back of the book before, when I was younger, but never thought much of it. The picture of the key was meaningless, just a doodle. The code seemed to mean nothing, but now I put all my effort into solving it. How could I have let a message from Mum sit on my shelf all these years?

I grab my notebook and pen from by the bed and sit down on the rug.

The first thing I note is that the string of Is, Vs and Xs can be broken down into Roman numerals –

IV IV XII V III X II IV III X II VII

Where to split some of the numbers is guesswork – the V and the III (five and three) could actually have been VIII (eight). But if I do it this way, there are twelve numbers, or three groups of four, which seems neat –

(IV IV XII V) + (III X II IV) + (III X II VII)

I wrack my brain – what kind of code would use sets of four? I'm blank for a second, but then it hits me – the object I'm holding is a book! The groups of four numbers could be references to chapters, pages, lines and words. And from words, you could make a message.

Quickly, I flip to the fourth chapter, then the fourth page of the chapter, then run my finger down to the twelfth line, and along to the fifth word.

'. . . the symptoms do not **develop** until early the next morning!'

The next two references share a page, I realise, turning to the tenth page of chapter three. I run my finger along the second line, and discover the other two words in the same sentence . . .

'I spent it **in** ransacking the **library** until I discovered a medical book, which gave me a description of strychnine poisoning.'

That's it, I have no more. The message is – 'Develop In Library'. I stare at it for a moment, my heart sinking. The message seems like nonsense. For a second I had a glimmer of hope. Not just that the puzzle was about to be solved, but that, after all these years, I was going to get one last message from Mum.

I slump back, my mind unfocused, letting disappointment flood in. Then, like a voice at the back of my head that won't shut up, the phrase keeps repeating itself to me.

Develop in library . . .

Develop in library . . .

Develop in library . . .

I look up to a spot on one of the highest shelves. The books up there have spent many years unread – they are of no interest to me. There are catalogues of other books, or treatises on 'information management', whatever that is. Then I see it – right there, in the middle of the shelf, sits one of Mum's old reference books – *Developments in Librarianship, Vol. 18*.

Trembling slightly, I pull a chair over to the shelf, get up, and take down the heavy brown book. My hand pauses for a second over the cover, almost not wanting to open it, scared of finding nothing inside. Surely that is what awaits me – another disappointment. Well, better to get it over and done with.

I open the book.

A small slip of paper – an old bookmark – falls out.

For a moment, I stop breathing altogether. There,

in the middle of the book, is no page at all. Someone has hollowed out the book with a knife, making a small, rectangular compartment. And there, gleaming darkly in the light, is a key. A perfect physical copy of the drawing – the black lines translated into wrought iron.

I take the key from the book. It is cold, heavy and real. It had belonged to my mother and, after many years, she has given it to me. I have no idea where it came from, or what it is supposed to open. But it is mine.

I take the key and get into bed, exhausted now.

I gaze at the puzzle one more time before switching off the lamp.

Despite the baking heat in my little attic room, I fall asleep in a matter of seconds, the strange key grasped in my hand.

8.

UNDER THE WEEPiNG TREE

It's Saturday, but I still wake before eight. I'm exhausted and groggy from the night before. But I wake with the key still cradled in my palm, and that makes me stop and think. Even though I don't know its purpose, the key is precious. I can't bring myself to put it down. I rummage through my jewellery box – a beautiful old Chinese box with an embroidered lid that belonged to Mum – and find one of Mum's silver chains, which I thread through the key and fasten round my neck.

I turn my radio on and listen to the news –

'... *further outbreaks of looting and rioting across*

London, as the water shortage worsens. Police have been called to an unplanned demonstration on Old Kent Road which is blocking traffic. Fire crews attending a blaze in Putney have been struggling to control the flames at a carpet warehouse with the limited water supplies . . .'

I shut it off, a hollow feeling in my stomach. The next thing I do is to send a message to Liam. I might not use my phone much, but Liam has to be alerted immediately. I send the words 'Custard Cream' – our standard code for an urgent rendezvous – and the number 12, which tells him that he needs to come to my house at noon.

I go downstairs and make some toast, and am walking back through to the living room when I see a note on the doormat. It's a plain envelope, without an address. All it says on the front is 'Agatha'. I pick it up, noting that there is something inside. Maybe I should go and put gloves and goggles on before opening it. But I can't wait.

I pull out a handwritten note, and something else falls to the floor. The note reads –

You shouldn't spy on people.

My heart is racing. Someone is trying to scare me off. I look down at what has fallen out – it's a wilted white flower. I look at it carefully, trying to understand what it means. Dad is the expert on flowers, not me, but I know the name of this one – clematis. It's the plant that is growing up the back wall of our house, underneath my window. I run through the kitchen, open the back door and go out into the garden.

There, under my window, the grass is covered in dozens of white flowers – each and every one of them has been cut away from the plant. Dozens of dead flowers, drying in the sun. Who would have done this? I shiver – whoever I'm dealing with, they know how to creep me out.

I think about the message – 'You shouldn't spy on people'. I remember hearing JP's voice, calling out to my dad. He's always been so friendly and unassuming, just living in the park. But could this be something to do with him? I realise how little I know about the mystery man. He came to live in the park a few months ago, and introduced himself to me. Dad went and talked to him and decided he was all right. But what did Dad know about him? What if JP has been spying on us all along?

I put the letter and the flower in evidence bags and put those up in my room. Then I clear up the flowers on the lawn – hopefully with everything going on, Dad won't notice that someone has decapitated his plant. I brush my hands off and take a deep breath. I'm not going to be intimidated – I have to get to the bottom of what is going on.

I'm just coming in through the back door when Dad shambles into the kitchen, still wearing his pyjamas (which is unusual for him, even at the weekend).

'Late night?' I ask, putting on the kettle.

'It –' Dad pauses for a big yawn – 'was.'

'You had a visitor?' I ask, trying not to sound too interested as I take two mugs from the cupboard and two teabags from the jar.

'Mmph.' Dad nods, sitting heavily at the table.

'Just some bloke from the Environment Agency, wanting to know how the park is getting on in the drought.'

'Oh, right. Did you tell him about your experiments?' The kettle clicks and I pour it out (NO. 1 DAD mug for him and an Eiffel Tower souvenir mug for me).

'Yeah, but there wasn't much to say. It's not like I know anything the Environment Agency doesn't. We ended up talking about you, actually.'

'About *me*?' A chill runs down my back.

'Yeah, just making conversation really. He said he has a daughter your age, and I was telling him that you want to be a detective when you grow up . . . Nice bloke, actually.'

I hand Dad his cup of tea, feeling queasy.

'I, uh, I should go . . . Things to do.'

'All right. Don't forget your homework this weekend – you'll feel better when it's done.'

'OK, Dad.'

I leave the kitchen and climb the stairs to my room. Perhaps the man's visit was just a coincidence, but I have a bad feeling. And why was JP lurking outside our house when he left? There are many questions and few answers, but I can't shake the sense that I'm being watched.

Gathering my thoughts, I go back to the mysterious key – what could it be for? What could it lead to? Whatever it is, it has to be important – Mum took the trouble to hide it, and left a coded message so I would find it. (*Eventually*, I think. I'm embarrassed at how long the key had lain there, undetected.) I pace the room, thinking over everything I know, but getting no further. I sit down on my bed and write a list of points in my notebook, which is filling up quickly –

1. The key was hidden, so it must be important.
2. If the key is important, it must open something.
3. Mum wanted me to find the key.

Tears prick my eyes, but I blink them away.

4. If so, she must have left something telling me what the key opens.

And yet – what can that clue be? I have no idea what the key might be for, or where I might find out. Then, out of the corner of my eye, I see something lying on the floor – a tiny slip of paper.

'Of course!' I shout, snatching up the bookmark that fell out of the book last night. In my excitement at discovering the key, I'd forgotten all about it. When I turn it over, I see it's a tiny photo. The image – a grainy black-and-white shot barely bigger than a passport photo – shows a caged-off tunnel. A path leads down to a small opening covered by iron bars. I know that tunnel, and search my memory for a moment. I have it – it's a tunnel in Hyde Park, at the edge of the Serpentine.

The tunnel must run right under the lake. I've always thought it was just some sort of drain.

'Right,' I say to myself, suddenly scared of what I know I must do next . . .

⌐○

An hour later, I'm striding down to the caged-off tunnel, dressed all in black and wearing gigantic wading boots, with a torch in one hand and a gas mask in the other. The gas mask came with our cottage – it had been sitting in its box under the stairs since the Second World War, quietly gathering dust. I don't know if it still works, but it will have to do. It's all I have to protect me from the noxious fumes of the red gunge. Most importantly, I have a set of keys to the grating in my pocket. In Dad's room, there's a rack holding dozens of sets of keys, for all kinds of sheds, gateways and grates around the park. It took me a little while to find the right one for the grating. It was labelled *Serpentine and Surrounds*. None of the keys look like the mystery key round my neck, but some of them are very old.

I go down the short ramp to the grate and look around, but nobody is there to see me. People aren't going out much, preferring to stay home and keep cool. Also, there are rumours that the red slime might cause all sorts of diseases if inhaled, so people are getting nervous about breathing in the city air.

According to the news, thousands of people have left to go to the countryside, and sales of air conditioning have gone through the roof.

I try a couple of Dad's keys in the padlock before I come to the right one. The lock clicks open in my hand. I take a deep breath and put on the gas mask. It smells musty, but I don't have any choice – there could be more of the noxious red slime down here. Switching on the torch, I step into the tunnel.

The space is tiny – I have to crouch right down to move through it. The floor is muddy concrete, the arched tunnel made of crumbling brick. Though I can't see any of the red slime yet, I can smell its familiar stink, and hope the gas mask is protecting me. I press on, not allowing myself to stop and think about what I'm doing. The tunnel seems to go on forever, until my legs are cramping and my neck stiff. The floor becomes muddier, and now there are pools of thick red algae. I tread carefully, my hand on the wall and my feet squelching in slime, but I can't see much through the tiny circles of glass in front of my eyes. Suddenly, my hand misses the wall and my feet slip from under me.

I curse as I hit the ground hard. I'm covered in the cold ooze. It makes my hands sting – I wish I'd thought to wear gloves. The torch jolts from my grasp and hits the ground with a clunk. I'm terrified its bulb will blow and leave me in darkness, but the light stays on. I take a moment to make sure I'm not badly hurt. I'm more winded than injured. I collect my torch and get up again. It can't be far now, I tell myself. On and on I go, becoming shaky and light-headed, as if I'm reaching high altitude, rather than a tunnel just a few metres below ground. Finally, the passage opens into a slightly taller tunnel that turns right. I stand, relief spreading through my aching muscles. Ahead of me is a narrow opening, like a doorway. When I shine the torch through it, no light bounces back – it must be a big cavern.

I take a deep breath, nervous but excited – I'm about to find something incredible, I'm sure.

Gripping the torch, I step though the gap, and out into –

Nothing.

I shine my light around, taking in the space. It's big, that much is true. I'm standing in a vast arch of brick under the Serpentine. The roof is leaky, dripping gobbets of slime. The floor is covered in water and algae, completely unusable. The whole place feels empty and abandoned. I stand there for a minute, jaw clenched inside the gas mask – whatever I expected to find under the lake, it isn't here. Was the clue a red herring? But why would Mum want to lead me on a wild-goose chase?

I'm turning to leave when the beam of my torch passes over something. I point it back, squinting through the greasy glass of the mask. It's just a patch of brown, a slightly different colour from the surrounding brick, and a little shorter than me. I squelch over to the wall, and as I get closer I can see that it's a door made of cast iron and rivets. The handle is a single bar that can't be turned. But below it there is a keyhole.

I don't know how I know, but I do. Perhaps the keyhole looks a similar shape. Perhaps it's just something about the door itself. Perhaps it's just my overactive imagination. Perhaps I have read *Alice in Wonderland* too many times. Whatever it is, I take the mystery key from round my neck and insert it into the lock. I turn the key, and a smooth, well-oiled mechanism goes – *click*!

Click.

Oh crikey.

It went click.

It clicked.

Feeling like I've walked into a dream, I pull on the handle and the door swings back smoothly. Golden light shines out, into the dank cave, smothering the tiny light of my torch.

I look down. At my feet is a doormat printed with the word 'WELCOME!'.

In front of the doormat stands a small umbrella holder, which is empty. And in front of that runs a plush red carpet, very clean and dry. I take off my gas mask and peer through the doorway. The carpet stretches in two directions down a long corridor illuminated by wall lights. The corridor has fine oak panelling on the walls, like the interior of a stately home. On a pedestal near the door sits a logbook and a pen. I look at the book, which seems to record times, identity numbers and the condition of the tunnel. It doesn't tell me what I need to know, so I flick to the front of the book.

The Gatekeepers' Guild – Inspection Log, No. 38261.

As I stare in disbelief at the ordinary objects in front of me – so out of context in this strange tunnel – I hear the sound of someone whistling down the corridor. I freeze for a second, and hear the soft tread of their shoes on the carpet. Very quickly, I retreat into the cavern, shut the heavy iron door and lock it, fingers fumbling with the key.

I stand there in darkness for a second, my breath rasping from the fumes, hoping that whoever is walking down the corridor didn't hear me. I press my ear to the cold iron. Faintly, I can hear the whistling behind the door. It stops, and I hold my breath. There is a pause, then the whistling resumes and fades away.

I stand alone in the darkness.

After another long walk back through the tunnels, I'm shaking with tiredness, begrimed with mud and slime from head to toe. I just want to get out. I emerge into the sunlight – birds are singing. I start to walk through the park, but my relief is cut short when I see a trio of girls under a tree. As I get closer, I see it is the CCs – Sarah, Ruth and Brianna – using the park as a place to take selfies.

Sarah shrieks when she sees me trudging across the lawns.

'What. The?' Ruth asks nobody in particular.

I peel off the gas mask to reveal my face.

'Is that . . . *Agatha*? You have *got* to be kidding me.'

'What are you doing in the sewers, Odd Socks?' Sarah taunts, horror replaced by glee. 'Meeting friends?'

Brianna just looks at me open-mouthed. Has she made peace so quickly with Sarah? She doesn't say anything *to* me, but she certainly doesn't say anything in my defence, either. The other two don't seem to notice her silence. I see that Sarah has a bottle of water in her hand. I wouldn't usually ask her for anything, but I'm desperate.

'Please, I'm so thirsty . . . Can I have some water?'

'Oh what, this?' She looks at the bottle in her hand. 'Sorry, this is for my spritzer.' She takes out a small spray-bottle, fills it with the last of the water, and sprays some on her face. 'You know, it's just so hard to keep *cool* in this heat,' she finishes, grinning evilly.

Ruth and Sarah's laughter rings out so loudly that I think the whole park will hear it, but I just walk past them without saying anything. I can still hear their laughter way off. For once, their insults don't hurt me – I've just discovered something huge, something quite impossible. Most importantly, I've discovered something that Mum *wanted* me to discover. Is this something to do with how she died? Or something else entirely? Either way, I need to find out more about the Gatekeepers' Guild.

By the time I'm out of the rubber waders, there is a knock at the front door – Liam has arrived on our doorstep. I open it and words come tumbling out of him.

'Agatha! Is everything OK? You sent the emergency signal – I would have come sooner, but you said twelve and I didn't want to mess up your plan if you had one . . .'

I hold up my hand to halt him.

'Liam, I'm fine. Sorry if I panicked you, but I have a lot to tell you.'

I think, after everything I've done, that I deserve a cup of tea. 'Just wait while I get changed.' I point to my black jeans and top, which are still soaked in slime from the tunnel.

'What have you been doing?' His eyes bug out.

'I'll tell you in a minute.'

I run upstairs and change quickly into a striped navy T-shirt with navy ankle-length Capri pants, a red belt and red lace-up pumps, and tuck Mum's key inside the neck of my top. I grab my notebook, then run back downstairs. I walk past Liam, towards the front door.

'Come on,' I tell him over my shoulder. 'We're going to the Orangery.'

'To the . . . but . . . hang on . . .' he splutters, following me out. I shoot him a radiant smile – for some reason, this always works. 'Oh, *all right*,' he says.

⌐○

The Orangery is an elegant tearoom next to Kensington Palace, at the west side of the park. We crunch up the gravel, past the Round Pond in front of the café, which is usually full of lily pads and water flowers, but now is scummed over with a red skin. There are normally tables outside the Orangery, but thanks to the stink coming off the pond, all the tables have been taken inside, the doors and windows shut. Liam pauses by one of the windows, which is hung with delicate lace.

'Are you sure about this? We could just get a couple of ice creams from the van.'

I drag him inside, and a tinkling bell above the door summons the maître d'. What I haven't told Liam is that I have a special relationship with Mr Worth, the head waiter at the Orangery, after I helped him out one day with a difficult customer. Ever since, he's always given me the broken meringues or less-than-perfect scones.

'Hello, Miss Oddlow!'

'Hello, Mr Worth.' I grin. 'A table for two, please.'

'Of course.' Mr Worth gives me a wink and leads me to a side table.

As ever, there is a heavenly glow in the café – the walls are pure white, with soaring Corinthian columns and flowing curtains. We are taken right through the interior, past rows of quietly spoken men in blazers and women in Chanel suits, and are seated out of the way, in one of the apses where King George II used to enjoy holding court.

'So, are you . . . all right?' Liam asks.

'Yes,' I say cautiously, realising that my brain is so full of new, confusing information that it's buzzing like a beehive. Maybe I'm not all right, actually – maybe I've discovered too many things all at once. 'Anyway, listen – I have a lot to tell you.'

At that moment, typically efficient, the tea arrives. I can see Liam shifting anxiously, wanting to hear my news, but I wait. Finally, the waitress is gone, I have poured myself a cup, put a sugar cube in, sipped the hot tea – and I am ready.

'So, last night . . .'

I start with the break-in that wasn't a break-in at Brianna's house and the revelation of her secret room. The scones and cream arrive with a pot of strawberry jam. I break off my story to spread clotted cream on to a scone and top it with a generous dollop of jam. I bite into it and can't help but smile at the taste. The head waiter has done us proud.

'Agatha!' Liam hisses, reaching for a scone. 'Stop making me wait!'

So I tell him about the mysterious visitor to our house last night, the discovery of the key, and my visit to beneath the Serpentine. I tell him about the Gatekeepers' Guild, and the secret passage, while Liam sits in silence, his undrunk cup of tea cooling in front of him, his eyes growing wider with each moment. When I'm done, he doesn't say anything. For a moment, he seems to have drifted off into a daydream.

'Liam?' I prod him in the ribs.

'What? Oh – sorry. It's a lot to absorb.'

'And? Don't you think it's incredible – a secret guild with tunnels under Hyde Park?'

He looks down into his tea, then up at me again. 'So who do you think the man at your house was?' He sounds concerned. I expected him to be amazed and excited, but his worry trumps any sense of adventure. I feel deflated.

'I'm not sure. Dad said he was some environmental officer . . .' I say, though I don't really believe it.

'Agatha, don't you think you should stop investigating? I don't want you to get hurt.'

'But, Liam, don't you see what's going on? We've stumbled across something huge. This shady organisation – "the Gatekeepers' Guild" – maybe they're the ones behind the red slime. Perhaps they're using their tunnels to infiltrate and poison London!'

'Maybe . . .' Liam sounds uncertain. 'But something doesn't stack up. Agatha, this is all too dangerous. That letter you got. This isn't a lost cat or a stolen bicycle. These people, whoever they are, must be powerful and, if you get in their way, they'll hurt you – they've made that clear. I can't let them do that.'

'Look, I'm not worried,' I tell him. 'This is bigger than my safety.'

'Well, if you're not worried for yourself, then what about your dad?'

I open my mouth to answer him, but nothing comes out. There is a heavy feeling in my stomach, an indigestible weight, like I ate a rock. He's right – investigating further could risk the safety of my father. Then I think about my mum. She had clearly wanted me to find the key, had wanted me to find the tunnel, had wanted me to *investigate*.

I can't let her down.

I open my mouth to tell Liam all of this, just as Mr Worth appears by my side, holding a silver platter.

'Ahem.' He coughs and winks.

He lowers the silver platter so that I can see the envelope resting on it. It's addressed in neat copperplate handwriting – *To Miss Agatha Oddlow*.

'Did you see anyone deliver this?'

Mr Worth shakes his head. I take the letter from the platter and wait for Mr Worth to leave.

'How does anyone even know you're here?' Liam asks me when the head waiter has gone.

'I was wondering the same thing.' I look down at the envelope in my hand, which has crashed our party like an uninvited guest.

'Open it, open it!'

'OK . . .'

Tearing into the envelope, I pull out a short note, written in the same immaculate calligraphy –

Dear Miss Oddlow,

Your intrusion has not gone unnoticed.

Perhaps you would care to find out more about us?

There are many bargains to be had among he South Bank bookstalls.

Yours,

The Gatekeepers' Guild

P.S. Best to shop alone.

I take a deep breath.

'The Gatekeepers' Guild?' says Liam in a whisper. 'The ones with the carpeted corridor under the Serpentine?'

I nod. 'It would seem so.'

9.

THE TURNiNG EYE

London's South Bank is a series of concrete buildings, underpasses and winding staircases. Some people think of it as an ugly growth on London's historic silhouette, but it's always been one of my favourite places. It almost seems that the Gatekeepers – whoever they are – know what I like. After all, they knew to find me at the Orangery. Tucked between the Waterloo and Hungerford railway bridges are table after table of secondhand books, laid out to lure me to spend more money than I have.

Liam didn't want me to accept the invitation in the note. He said it was too dangerous. But when he realised that I was going and he couldn't stop me, he said he'd come along.

'Liam, it says "best to shop alone" – they don't want anyone to accompany me.'

'And that's exactly what worries me!' He adjusts his glasses in frustration. 'Because if you're on your own, they're free to drag you off to who-knows-where!'

'But if you're there, they may not show themselves at all.'

'And . . .' He shrugs.

I sigh – he isn't making this easy for me.

'Do you think you can protect me from whatever happens, Liam?'

He thinks about this seriously for a moment. 'Nope. Not at all, actually. But we're mates and I want to do my best to look after you.'

I bristle – since when do I, Agatha Oddlow, need *looking after*?

He realises what he's said almost immediately. 'I mean . . . we can keep an eye out. Together. Can't we?'

I give up. 'Fine. You can come along. But try to blend in.'

'Sure.' He shrugs, pulling his arms and legs in as though trying to vanish behind a lamppost. I laugh before I can stop myself.

We walk. The Serpentine still has its floating islands of red algae. Hyde Park is much quieter than usual for a Saturday, almost deserted. We pass occasional walkers, all wearing masks against the algae's noxious gases. Doctors in the seventeenth century wore masks filled with flowers, believing the sweet scent would protect them from the plague – I wonder if these masks really protect people from the fumes. There aren't any joggers, as there usually would be, perhaps because there's just not enough water to waste on having a shower afterwards.

I'm finding the going tough – it's hot and I've inhaled a lot of fumes. I try not to picture my bedroom, with its sloping ceiling, my rows of books and my picture of Mum. Most of all, I try not to picture my bed, to imagine climbing back into it and letting my head slump against the pillow.

We walk through Knightsbridge, down the Mall and up past Buckingham Palace. I wonder how the Queen feels about the shortage of water, although I feel sure she's probably not going without. After half an hour of walking, we cross the Thames by the Golden Jubilee footbridge. Often, the wind here is strong and cold, but today the breeze lifting off the Thames is a relief. The river has a spattering of the red slime here and there, which has escaped from the underground rivers. My throat feels dry and I'm desperately thirsty.

'Nearly there,' says Liam.

We both slow down as we cross the bridge. It's impossible not to be struck by the London skyline – the magnificent dome of St Paul's, the white filigree of the London Eye, the arches of Charing Cross Station ... even the rocket-ship sheen of the Gherkin. In my eagerness to reach our destination and have something to drink I almost throw myself down the steps to the South Bank. I stumble at a bend in the staircase, and Liam grabs my elbow.

'Steady!'

When I reach the lower level, I sink on to the nearest bench to the book stalls.

'Must sit. Need drink,' I admit. My lungs feel bruised.

'Wait here.' Liam runs into the Royal Festival Hall. Three brightly coloured slides have been installed outside, and families gather as children climb the steps and come down the slides over and over again, shouting, 'Wheeeee!' The children are the only ones who don't seem to understand what's going on. Everyone else in the capital wears a scared, what's-going-to-happen-next look on their face.

At that moment, Liam reappears at a run, clutching an orange ice lolly.

'They're out of water.'

'No surprises. Thanks, though.'

I take the lolly and rip off the paper, biting huge chunks out of the ice. It's gone all too soon.

'Ready to go?' Liam asks.

'Just about.' I point to the book stalls. 'I'll look at the books, but I don't want them to spot you.'

'You think they might be watching us?'

'I have no idea, but stay here just in case.'

'OK . . . and you just stay where I can see you, OK?'

I go over to the first of the long book tables and look for anything that might be a clue. It's an antiquarian stall – most of the books have hard covers in dark colours, with gilt lettering across the front and down the spine. I pick up *Great Expectations* by Charles Dickens. The edges of the pages are ragged where they were sliced apart by the first reader, in the days before books came with their pages already separated. I hold it to my nose and breathe in the old-book smell.

'Are you going to buy that?' The stall owner – a tall man with a pronounced Adam's apple, is frowning at me.

I smile sweetly. 'I'd love to, but I can't possibly afford it.'

'Then put it down,' he says without humour. 'These are precious – not to be sniffed at by random passersby.'

I move on. Every so often I glance across at Liam, who's watching me like a hawk (while trying to look like he's not watching me) from the bench. Any of the people around us could be one of the mysterious Gatekeepers.

I'm so distracted that I hardly notice the book at first. But then the name catches my attention. I pick it up and gasp.

In my hands is a hardback copy of Agatha Christie's *Poirot Investigates*. If this is a first edition, then it's worth a fortune.

Liam must see my excitement, because he carefully makes his way over. I'm so shocked I forget that we're supposed to be staying separate.

'What is it?'

'This . . .' I begin, barely able to get the words out. My hands are trembling as I open it up to see that I am right. My voice is low and reverent. 'This is the rare 1924 edition of *Poirot Investigates*, with the first ever picture of Hercule Poirot on the dust jacket.'

He glances at the book, then back to me. 'That's . . . nice?'

'Nice? *Nice*, Liam? A copy was sold at auction recently, and it fetched –' I lower my voice to a whisper – 'more than £40,000!'

Liam's eyes bulge and his mouth falls open. The book is among the faded old paperbacks and celebrity memoirs, almost as though it has been placed there. I have so many questions I don't know where to start.

'You should look inside,' Liam says.

I gently turn the pages of the book, searching. There's a scrap of paper and two tickets just inside the back cover. 'This is it!'

The slip of paper has two things on it – the number 33 and the words 'You might as well bring your friend, now he's here'.

'Well, so much for blending in.' Liam grins. 'What's that number all about?'

It would mean nothing to me, except that the two tickets that are with it are for the London Eye.

'I think I know,' I say. 'Follow me.'

'But what about the book—'

Liam is cut short by a voice close by and we both jump.

'I'll make sure it gets back to its rightful owner.' It's the stallholder, a woman with blue hair and a nose piercing. She winks at me as reluctantly I hand back the book.

'Quite something, isn't it?' she says, gently stroking the cover before placing the book in a velvet-lined box.

'It certainly is.' I turn to Liam. 'Now, come on, let's go.'

We don't queue when we reach the wheel; I just produce the tickets and we are ushered through the express lane and soon find ourselves standing at the base of the giant structure. I watch the transparent capsules travel slowly round on the wheel's axis, forgetting my exhaustion. But when the first pod empties of passengers and the steward nods for us to embark, I shake my head.

'We'll wait, if that's all right.'

The steward seems unsure, but after a moment's hesitation he shrugs, turning his attention to the long queue of tourists.

'What are we waiting for?' asks Liam.

'Pod number thirty-three, of course.'

Finally, pod thirty-three comes round. I grab Liam and walk in. The Eye doesn't stop to let people on. Rather, it moves slowly enough that you can just hop on. The pod is empty. I sit down on the bench in the centre and examine the capsule. There's nothing unusual about it – like all the pods, it's an ovoid glass room, with a pale, polished floor and an oval wooden bench in the centre.

'Hang on . . .' Liam says. 'Aren't there only thirty-two pods? I read about it – thirty-two pods for the thirty-two boroughs of London.'

'Yeah, but there's no number thirteen. So there's a number thirty-three to make up for the missing pod,' I say.

'That's right,' says a woman's voice, and I turn in surprise.

There's no one there, of course, but a screen fixed to the side rail of the pod has lit up. But instead of telling us about the London skyline, or the ride we're on, it just shows a woman.

Dorothy D'Oliveira.

She's leaning slightly on a wooden stick. 'So, number thirteen is unlucky,' she snorts, 'if you believe in such nonsense.'

'What . . .?' I turn in confusion to Liam, but he's looking just as baffled.

'You found the book, then,' she says, her voice tinny over the intercom. She chuckles. 'Just a little joke of mine. I know how much you enjoy the works of your namesake. And that was an extra-special edition, wasn't it?'

'I didn't want to give it back,' I admit, trying to understand what is going on. I can't tell where the professor is – she's standing against a black background that gives nothing away.

'I trust you did give it back, though?' she asks.

I nod.

'Good,' she continues, 'or that would have been a rather large claim on my expense account.' She looks Liam up and down. 'I did ask you to come *alone*, didn't I, Agatha?'

'You did.' Liam is sheepish. 'But I insisted on coming too,' he says. 'I was worried . . .'

Professor D'Oliveira nods. 'Good friend. Well, Liam, my name is Dorothy D'Oliveira. Agatha may have mentioned me.' The professor smiles, but I don't smile back. From this meeting, it's clear that there is a lot the professor hasn't been telling me. I have no reason to trust her, to give away what I know. Liam is silent.

'Why have you called me here? Do you have information?'

'Not exactly,' Professor D'Oliveira says. 'And, actually, I wouldn't usually do this, Miss Oddlow. But you've seen my face, and you've made some . . . *connections*.' She looks away from the camera, staring off at whatever view is behind her. 'A little knowledge is a dangerous thing, so I want to give you a few more facts to think about.'

'*Now* you want to tell me the facts?' I say. 'You didn't seem overly keen to talk to me the last time we met.'

She laughs and looks at Liam, who is at the edge of the pod. 'I like this girl,' she says to him. 'She tells it like it is.'

I sigh impatiently. We are nearing the top of the ride, and will soon start our descent. We don't have a lot of time. 'Who is "we", anyway? And where did you get your tattoo?' I ask.

'That's a whole lot of questions, Agatha.' A long pause follows.

I huff. 'I thought you were going to start giving me answers.'

She smiles. 'I was, but Liam being here as well has . . . Well, it's thrown me a bit.'

'Whatever you want to say, you can say in front of my friend.'

'I'll have to take your word for that . . .' She takes a deep breath, as if thinking it all through, and then she seems to come to a decision. 'The tattoo,' she starts, 'is a symbol for an organisation – a secret organisation – called the Gatekeepers' Guild.'

I force my face to remain expressionless but an electric tingle shoots down my spine at the mention of that name – the name from the secret tunnel.

'Some people carry the symbol in their wallet, or have it sewn into the lining of their blazer. Wherever they feel it's *discreet*.' She arches her eyebrow at me. 'Personally, I wanted something more permanent, and since I wear long sleeves . . .' She pushes her sleeve back to reveal the silvery tattoo – the one I first saw in the park that day.

'Why now?' I ask. 'Why are you telling me all this? What's changed since the hospital, when you pressed the emergency buzzer to have me evicted?'

'Don't you know?' she asks.

'No idea,' I say, trying to reach deep into the recesses of my brain for something that seems to just be lingering there, struggling to make its way to the surface.

'Well, you stumbled a little too close for comfort . . .' The professor folds her hands neatly. 'So, to keep it brief – the Guild has members all over London. Gatekeepers, both literally and figuratively. The majority of our members, in their roles as caretakers, housekeepers, butlers and so on, hold keys to the ancient buildings that are an integral part of London.'

'Waiters too?' I raise an eyebrow, thinking how Mr Worth had handed me that letter at the Orangery.

'Perhaps,' Professor D'Oliveira says. 'Anyway, these buildings, and their grounds, offer access to the tunnels that run all over the city beneath its inhabitants' feet.'

I think about Dad's rack of keys that open all the grilles and gates in the park. 'So . . . Dad? Is that why he has so many keys?'

She shakes her head. 'Not your father. He was never a member.'

I open my mouth to ask 'then who?', but she holds up a hand to silence me.

'I don't have time for all of your questions right now, but let me at least explain a bit more, and then you can ask later.'

I nod as Professor D'Oliveira starts again. 'The Gatekeepers are custodians of this country,' she says, 'and have been for centuries. We're secret agents. We get the cases that MI5 can't solve. When everyone else is stuck, we step in.'

I suck in a deep breath as she looks me in the eye. 'What you saw – the assault on my person in Hyde Park – has put you in danger. Now, I need you to listen to me, and do as I say.'

'And why should I trust you? How do I know that you're on the right side in whatever's going on?'

She laughs. 'Because there's no one else you can trust to help you.' She leans in more closely to the camera. 'The truth is, you can walk out of here and pretend that this chat never happened, but then you'd be on your own. And believe me, the people who are coming after you are a whole lot tougher than me. What you saw – well, that's just the start.'

'Why are you telling me all this?' I ask. 'Why would your secret organisation bother itself with a thirteen-year-old girl?'

The professor doesn't say anything. She just stares at me. She isn't telling me something, but I feel like I already know what it is. The key stashed in my room, the clues left for me to find – all from Mum. She wouldn't have left them for me if she thought they would lead me into danger. She left them because she wanted me to find out about the Guild.

'My mum,' I say. 'My mum was a member, wasn't she? She was a member of the Gatekeepers' Guild!'

The professor has closed her eyes. Even over the scratchy intercom, I can hear her take a deep breath.

'Your mother was one of our agents, yes,' she says quietly. 'One of *my* agents. The best.'

The pod seems to contract around me. The view of Parliament and the river swims dizzyingly. There's a roaring sound in my ears.

'What?' My voice has gone very small.

The professor nods. 'Clara was incredible. Does that really surprise you?'

'No, but . . .' I remember the key round my neck. 'Well, it's a shock.'

'I'm sure. But it's the truth.'

'So can I join and take her place?' I ask, feeling a lump rise in my throat. Where did that come from? The words were out of my mouth before I had time to think about them.

Professor D'Oliveira's eyebrows shoot up. 'It's not as simple as that – there isn't anyone as young as you in the Guild, for starters, and, even if there was, there are tests to complete.'

'Tests? What kind of tests?'

'Enough for now . . .' Professor D'Oliveira spoke. 'We can't just let anyone into the Guild.'

I cross my arms. 'But I'm not "just anyone".'

'I can see that. And perhaps some day that will change, but in the meantime I'm asking you not to meddle – to leave it to the experts to deal with this crisis.'

'You mean . . . the water? The red slime?'

She frowns, saying nothing, but for a secret agent she's quite transparent.

'I knew it! I knew it wasn't just an accident!'

'Agatha, listen to me – you need to forget what you know.'

Forget what I know? How can I do that?

'Agatha, we have to get off in a moment,' says Liam, eyeing the ground below as the capsule slowly approaches the end of its circuit.

'Yes, and this is the end of our conversation for now,' the professor says.

I feel as though I'm going to cry with frustration. I've learnt so much but at the same time, so little. I force the tears back.

'One last thing, Agatha – look after your father. He is too trusting.'

The screen goes blank.

Then it switches on again. 'Oh, and, Agatha?'

'Yes?'

'Stay *out* of our tunnels.'

The intercom shuts off for good. The pod draws level with the ground, and the steward asks us to step off. Liam and I move away from the wheel.

'Well, that's that,' he says.

'What's what?'

'The end of your investigation.'

'What? What are you talking about?' I spin round angrily.

'This is serious, Agatha – you have to stop. You heard what she said – there are people who might come after you – people who could cause you serious harm.'

The blood is rising in my cheeks.

'My mum was involved in all of this. I'm not going to stop! Not until I get some answers.'

Liam kicks hard at an empty drinks can, which

skitters off into the crowds. 'Don't you care what I think?' he says.

'Of course I care what you think,' I shout. 'But look, Liam, this is important . . .'

Liam hangs his head. I've never seen him looking so hangdog or glum. He starts walking past the aquarium, heading for Westminster Bridge. 'I'll get us a cab then. Let's go up to the road.'

'I can make my own way, if you'd rather be on your own,' I huff.

He reels to face me. 'Did you not hear anything the professor said to you, about how much danger you're in? Agatha, you're so *stubborn*!'

Anger flares like a flame in my chest. 'How can you talk to me like that? After everything I just found out?'

'Somebody has to.'

'You are so arrogant,' I shout. 'You think you're in charge of me? That you can just boss me around?'

'*I'm* arrogant? You're the super-genius detective – I'm just some dopey sidekick to you. *Oh, Agatha, how fascinating! Oh, Agatha, you're sooo clever!'*

'Oh, yeah – I'm such a golden girl. Agatha Oddball, Oddity, Odd Socks . . . I'm a really difficult act to follow, aren't I?' I feel hot tears prickle at the back of my eyes.

'That's not who you are, Agatha.' Liam stops and takes a deep breath. We're blocking a group of tourists, who navigate around us. 'Those names have nothing to do with the real you. I don't mean to be so angry. It's just . . .'

'I know,' I say. 'I get it.'

'Taxi home, then?'

'Taxi home,' I agree.

⚷

In the cab, I'm dying to discuss the revelations about the Guild – and my mother – to see if Liam thinks the professor is trustworthy. But I don't want to make him feel even worse, so we sit in silence. The taxi is soon depositing me at the gates to Hyde Park.

'Take care,' he says.

'Thanks,' I say, climbing out. I watch the taxi drive off. Liam's face is blank at the window. For the first time I feel a rift open between us. The tears I've been holding back spill out. *Dumb*, I think to myself, wiping my cheeks.

By the time I reach our cottage, I've stopped feeling so tearful, but I'm still miserable. Through the front door I call out to Dad, but there's no answer. I don't like the way the house echoes. I peer into the kitchen, where his algae samples are bubbling away, like a mad scientist's lab. I hunt for Dad, the professor's words ringing in my ears – *Look after your father. He is too trusting.*

To my relief, I find Dad in the living room, fast asleep on the sofa, fully dressed and snoring loudly. Oliver is curled up on his lap, purring like a lawnmower. I don't want to wake him – he looks exhausted.

Apart from the ice lolly, I haven't eaten since the Orangery. I rummage for some bread and cheese in the kitchen, and take the food and a small glass of water up to my bedroom. Dad has brought back a gallon bottle of water from the shops, but it cost him as much as a week's shopping usually does.

I sit on my bed and start to drift off.

The film projector is in front of me again, shining memories on to my bedroom wall. I watch the film of my day for a long time, seeing myself on the London Eye, talking with Liam on the South Bank, being in the capsule . . . The images replay in front of me, but it doesn't help me think. My mind flicks back, swapping today for a day seven years ago. I see Mum pottering around the kitchen, swaying a little in time to the radio, buttering slices of toast for my breakfast.

Here is the quiet woman who introduced me to Agatha Christie and Hercule Poirot and I'm grateful that I can still see her like this – that the images haven't fled from my memory. And I know that the professor is telling me the truth about her. Mum might have been quiet, but she was anything but ordinary. I feel a bubble of excitement fizz up inside me. Mum. *My* mum. My totally amazing, kind, loving mum had been a secret agent.

I'm running through the silent corridors of St Mary's hospital. Turning left and right through the maze, I see figures standing in the shadows out of the corner of my eye. There are quick footsteps behind me. They are going to catch me, but I have to reach my destination first. The hospital is so dark. Finally, I push open the door to a room. This is the place I was searching for – Dad's room. He's in a hospital bed like the professor's, but he's unmoving, kept alive by machines. The door behind me opens . . .

I wake gasping, sitting bolt upright, as though someone has been holding me underwater. I wait for my heart to slow. The bad dreams all blend together, but the fear they leave behind stays with me. I creep down to the first floor and put an ear to Dad's door. I'd intended to wake him up after my snack and make sure he got into bed, but I must have dozed off myself. Thankfully, I see that he's made it off the sofa and up to bed at some point, and is now snoring loudly. I resist the childish urge to wake him up.

I'm torn. In my daydreams there are no consequences to solving a crime. You either get it wrong, or you get it right. But the real world isn't like my dreams – there are risks at every turn.

I have a quick breakfast of toast with marmalade and make up a buttered roll with cheese for JP. If JP is spying on us for some reason, I should pretend that I haven't noticed. As the old saying goes – *keep your friends close and your enemies closer*. I make myself a small cup of peppermint tea, scrawl a note for Dad and prop it in front of the toaster –

Off to visit Mum.

Dad will know what I mean.

⌐○

In the park, JP is nowhere to be seen. I hold the roll in my hand, as though it might summon him from his hiding place. Curious, I check his usual haunts – an oak tree near the lake, a bench surrounded by rhododendron bushes, and the railings by a patch of swaying poppies. Finally, I go to see if he's in the hollow of the famous upside-down tree. A huge weeping beech, the upside-down tree's branches hang down to the ground, making a sort of cave inside.

I crouch down to a gap in the branches and crawl into the darkened space. The air is oven-warm and smells of dry earth. This is a good place to hide in a rainstorm, for a while at least, until the rain bleeds through the canopy. There is nobody in here and I'm about to crawl back out when I glimpse a dark-red object among the roots of the ancient tree. It's a notebook. Crawling closer, I tug on the notebook, which comes free with a dusting of soil. There's a ballpoint pen stuck in the spiral binding. I look around, but I'm alone.

Only the first page of the notebook has anything on it.

22:43 – Arrived at house.

23:07 – Left house.

02:00 – Cutting flowers.

My heart speeds up. These notes are about me. Or, at least, about Dad and his mysterious visitor.

The first two timings are obvious to me – this was when Davenport had turned up at our house and when he had left. The third time is less clear, but the note must refer to the person who had cut all the flowers off the clematis under my window.

Who could this notebook belong to? If it's JP's, then is he spying on us, and, if so, who for? Was JP the person who had cut all the flowers? Whatever the truth, I'm creeped out by the thought of someone watching our house.

I close the notebook, replace it in the root hollow, and crawl out again.

⌐○

It takes me about half an hour's walk before the black metal railings of the cemetery come into view, with the two red phone boxes like sentries on either side of the gates. I'm hot and thirsty, but I'm on a mission.

There are a lot of famous people buried in Brompton Cemetery – and Mum. I think Mum would have liked the thought of being buried alongside the suffragette Emmeline Pankhurst, opera singers and boxers, the inventor of the Christmas card and Native Americans from *Buffalo Bill's Wild West* show.

Mum's grave is small and discreet. I'm sure that to anyone else it would look plain, like it doesn't belong to a person at all, but only a name. Even I have to look at it carefully, almost squint, until I can picture her in her tortoiseshell glasses, and smell the fruit cakes that she baked each week. Then it isn't a grey slab of stone any more, but a dusty grey window, to which I can press my face and glimpse her reading a book or dancing around the kitchen with the radio on, in another world altogether.

I sit down on the cool stone like I'm sitting on the edge of someone's bed.

'Hey, Mum . . .' I start, feeling lost for words. It might seem strange to some people, talking to someone who can't talk back. But Dad always says that Mum was a good listener, so I don't think she would mind.

'Sorry I haven't been for a while; it's been a strange week. Oh, but I did bring you this . . .'

I take a crime novel out of my bag that I'd picked up in a charity shop on the way, and place it on the stone. The one I left last time is still there, so I put that back in my bag. Sometimes they are soaked with rain, and sometimes they are gone altogether, but it feels more right to me than bringing flowers.

I sit for a minute in silence, not thinking about anything much. Then, when I feel ready, I start to talk about everything that has happened. I talk about the hit-and-run, Professor D'Oliveira and the strange tattoo. I talk about the faceless man who attacked me, and the red slime that's spreading all over London. I talk about Brianna, Liam and the professor warning me not to get involved. And, of course, I talk about the key – the present that she left me, and which I've finally found.

'I knew you had a secret, Mum . . . I just *knew* it.'

I'm talking and, out of nowhere, I start to cry. Maybe it's because talking about everything makes it seem more real. Maybe it's because I start to remember how scared I was when I was attacked. But mostly I think it's because I miss my mum.

As I cry, and the tears fall on the dusty stone, I feel a sinking tiredness come over me. The world turns sideways, until I'm resting my head on the grave, which seems as comfortable as my bed at home.

'You shouldn't be scared, you know.' She brushes my hair with her hand. My face is buried in the pillow so I can't see her.

'I just . . . I feel like this is what I'm supposed to do.' I sniff. The pillow smells of her perfume – a scent I'd almost forgotten.

'But . . .?' She coaxes.

'But . . . but I don't want anyone to get *hurt.*'

She sighs, and for the first time she sounds sad. 'Oh, sweetie, people always get hurt. That's the way life is. But to not live life to the full . . . Well, that's worse, I think.'

Her hand is soft, and my shoulders hunch up, like the feeling you get when you know you've got nothing left to cry. I raise my head from the pillow to look at her.

'Thanks, Mum . . .'

I look around me but no one is there. I'm in the

cemetery, and the grave is a grave, not a bed. The stone is still wet with my tears. I sit up and wipe my eyes. Something has changed, and it takes me a moment to realise what it is. The heavy weight in my heart has lifted.

'Thanks, Mum,' I repeat.

10.

THE FACE OF TOMORROW

'Morning, love.' Dad shuffles into the kitchen, yawning and stretching. It's Monday and already I feel like a different person from the day before. 'You making breakfast?' he asks.

I nod and grin. 'I thought we could both use it.'

I take the frying pan off the stove and divide the eggs, sausages and mushrooms between the two plates. The toast pops up on cue. I've begun to discover that, in times of stress, the best thing I can do is keep busy. Being still for just a moment feels like a strange paralysis. Dad sinks into a chair, sighing.

'Smells great.'

I present the plate of food and coffee, which has used up the last of our fresh water. Dad eats quietly, while I alternate between bites of my breakfast and cleaning up the kitchen as best I can without water.

'Don't you want to sit while you eat?' he asks at last.

'Just . . . tidying,' I say. 'Don't want to get in the way of your experiments.' I try to sound as cheery as possible, but only get another sigh from Dad.

'Oh, don't worry about them. I'll be chucking the lot down the sink today anyway.'

'Oh?' I am surprised. 'Why? What's happened?'

Dad shrugs and looks despondent. 'Happened? Take a look – they've all died, that's what.'

I peer in at them over the counter. The algae are all shrivelled up to a tiny mass. 'Isn't that a *good* thing?' I say.

'No – I was trying to keep the algae alive, in captivity, to find out what it eats. If I can find that out, I'd know how it's growing underground, in the ruddy dark!' Dad gets up and takes the lid off a blacked-out fish tank. I go over to join him and peer in. It's full of brown sludge.

'What *is* that?'

'This is what the algae look like when they run out of energy – the stuff in the Serpentine is going the same way.'

I poke the sludge with a spoon, making sure it's dead. It smells gross like old rotten eggs.

'So it doesn't feed on sunlight, or other plants, or animals . . . How can it still be growing and coming up through people's pipes?'

Dad slumps back into his chair with a grunt. 'That's exactly what I'd like to know. I'll leave science to the scientists from now on.'

We get ourselves clean as best we can, using wet wipes, and I hurry off to school.

As I walk down Kensington Road, chaos is all around me. A line of police cars and ambulances speed past, sirens blaring. A convoy of tankers and Green Goddess fire engines head in the other direction, bearing water into the dried-up city. But no quantity of water is going to be enough – the biggest convoy in the world can't replace the millions of miles of pipe that are now clogged with slime.

A crowd is marching towards Parliament Square, people with placards and megaphones, shouting and blowing whistles. They're calling for more to be done about the water shortage, and for controls to be put on the price of bottled water.

From a side street I can see people running, boxes under their arms. They've clearly looted them and are being chased by police officers. Looking closer, I can see the writing printed on the cardboard – not televisions or computers, but bottles of mineral water. It's a really desperate situation that we're in. I look down at the pavement and walk on. There's a tension in the air, you can really feel it, and I almost jump out of my skin when someone calls my name.

'Agatha! Hang on.'

I turn – it's Brianna Pike. What's she doing here? She's sprinting the short distance to me, hair streaming behind her like the ears on a golden retriever. She's wearing a blue jacket instead of her school blazer, and smiles in welcome. But I'm not ready to forgive her silence in the park.

'Hey . . .' I say slowly.

If she notices my coldness, she doesn't show it.

'Hey. Mind if I walk with you? Things are kind of crazy at the moment.'

'Sure.' I'm not sure if she means that London is crazy, or that Brianna Pike walking to school with Agatha Oddlow is crazy. 'Don't you normally get a lift?' I ask.

She shrugs. 'Couldn't drag my brother out of bed this morning to drive me, and my parents are still away.'

'Doesn't your brother work?'

'Not for much longer, if he keeps refusing to get up. Dad got him a trainee job with our uncle – something to do with –' she wrinkles her nose, as if in thought – 'diamonds? Or gold? I don't know. But Sebastian's meant to be in work at, like, nine in the morning, and he keeps sleeping through his alarm. He is *so* going to get fired.'

'Won't your dad go mad at that?'

She rolls her eyes and flicks back her honey-coloured hair. 'Totally. Mummy and Daddy call us every night, but Sebastian just pretends he's going into the office on time. I don't know how he thinks he'll get away with it.'

She looks sideways at me, and then asks a question that takes me by surprise –

'Anyway, what are you reading at the moment? I'm just finishing this book about unsolved London murders from the 1920s and 30s . . .'

'Hey, I've read that book! It's got the stabbing of the acrobat, Martial Chevalier, in Piccadilly, right?'

'Exactly! And the case of the unidentified body parts found at Waterloo Station.' With her long strides, Brianna is walking slightly ahead of me. Now, she stops and turns to face me and I stop quickly. 'So what age were you when you first got interested in investigating?'

I shrug. 'I don't know. Maybe six or seven.'

'Six or seven?' She shakes her head and goes back to walking. 'So I've got a lot of catching up to do! I didn't start till I was eleven. Eleven!'

I couldn't believe what I was hearing. Brianna? By the time we're nearing St Regis, I've forgotten all about my bad feelings towards her. We come to a halt just short of the school gates.

'Well, uh, I'm just going to stop here and check my make-up,' she says.

I hesitate, about to offer to wait, then I realise what's just happened – it's fine to talk to me *out* of school, but Brianna doesn't want to be seen with me once we're inside. I raise an eyebrow. 'Seriously?'

'What?'

I shake my head. 'Whatever. See you around, maybe.'

Again, she seems to miss my tone. 'That would be cool.' She smiles, pulling out a compact and dabbing her nose.

I shrug and walk away from her. As I make my way into the playground, I see bottles of water being handed out by men and women wearing branded uniforms. The words 'Alpha Aqua' are emblazoned on their aprons. Of course, there's no crisis so bad that someone isn't making money out of it. I see Liam in the crowd and wave to him.

He looks away.

What's going on? Liam has never ignored me before. Whenever I've investigated things before,

Liam has encouraged me. Now, I'm trying to solve a mystery much bigger than last year's 'Who stole Bernie Sipowicz's lunch money?' and Liam seems to be getting cold feet. Why can't he trust me to look after myself?

'Hey, Oddlow!' A voice shouts over the crowd. I can tell it's Ruth Masters, without even so much as looking round. 'You look like you haven't showered in weeks. Nothing new there, though, is there?'

Everyone within earshot laughs. I feel a flush of anger, but pretend not to have heard. St Regis students look after themselves a lot better than people on the street but even so, the people I saw on my walk to school looked as grimy and thirsty as me. They were quiet and careful not to use more energy than they had to.

'Agatha!' A familiar voice speaks behind me. I spin round, ready for another insult. It's Brianna again. But she isn't in CC mode this time – her smile is friendly, not mocking.

I still haven't quite forgiven her for stopping just

outside the school gates. 'What is it, Brianna?' I say.

'Have you seen these?' She's holding one of the water bottles in her hand and passes it to me. I take the bottle, realising how thirsty I am.

'Are you sure?' I ask.

'Go ahead . . .' Brianna nods. 'I've had plenty.'

I open the bottle and swallow the cold water in one long gulp. I get a brain freeze, but feel so much better. I look at the empty bottle with a twinge of guilt. Maybe I should have saved some to take home to Dad.

Brianna hands me a flyer. 'Look, they're handing out these leaflets with the bottles.'

'So? They just want free publicity, don't they? Handing out bottles of water to thirsty schoolkids – looks good in the paper.'

I look round and, sure enough, there's a photographer taking snaps of the bottles and all of us glugging them back. I hope my picture doesn't appear in the paper.

'Read here . . .' Brianna goes on. *'Alpha Aqua has recently built a world-class water-purification centre in London, providing jobs to thousands of local* yadda yadda . . .'

I frown, but my mind is already lighting up, hearing what Brianna is subtly trying to tell me. Casually, I say – 'You think it's too much of a coincidence?'

'A coincidence?' Brianna puts her hands on her hips. 'All of London is hit by a water shortage of biblical proportions, right after a London company has built *the largest water-purification centre in the Northern Hemisphere?*'

'You're right . . .' I nod. And then I remember. 'Alpha Aqua . . . AA! Like the pencil found at the scene of the hit-and-run!' I think for a second. 'Can you look the company up on your phone?'

'Sure.' Brianna smiles, taking out her smartphone. For the time being at least, she doesn't seem to be bothered about being seen with me. I take a moment to look around the playground, shifting my brain into top gear. Words appear, stitched in golden letters on to the backs of people's blazers as they move through the crowd . . .

ALPHA AQUA

Free Water

New Company?

Why St Regis?

Just what is it all about? My mind can't quite piece it all together.

'Oh, look!' Brianna shows me her phone, which has a news story on the screen. 'These Alpha Aqua guys are going to be giving a press conference at the Barbican Centre conservatory *today*.'

I look at the story – the press conference is at ten. I feel the excitement pumping through my veins and turn to my new-found friend.

'Want to go?'

Brianna looks up at me, startled. 'What, now? With you?'

I feel cross for a moment, then stop myself. I want to give her the benefit of the doubt. She might not have meant it to come out the way it sounded. 'Sure.' I hesitate. 'With me.'

'I don't know if I should . . .' But she's grinning lopsidedly – I can tell she wants to come. 'What about Liam? Wouldn't you normally ask him to go with you?'

'He's . . . busy today. Come on – we can do some *proper* investigating.'

She says nothing for a second, takes a shaky breath, then nods.

⌐○

I know I shouldn't be sneaking out of school again – Dad warned me – and sneaking someone else out with me is twice as bad. But I'm having too much fun, and yes – I want Brianna to be my friend.

My bin-escape-route isn't going to work today – not when I've already used it so recently – so we'll have to leave before the school gates close and we're trapped, which means we can't go to form class. I go first, walking out of the gates and a little way down the road. Brianna follows after, so we don't look so suspicious. People are still coming in and out of the school gates, so nobody notices us go. As soon as we're sure that nobody is following us, we start to run.

'I . . . can't believe . . . I'm doing this!' Brianna says between gasps, grinning from ear to ear.

We get on the tube and ride the Central line to Liverpool Street. The carriage is as hot as a sauna – everyone else is silent, cooling themselves with electric fans and newspapers. I see the headlines, and they're all about the red slime.

'*Water Crisis – Prime Minister Calls for Calm.*'

'*Top Scientists Search for Algae Cause.*'

'*"I Can Stop the Slime!" Says TV Psychic.*'

Me and Brianna chat all the way, looking over the pamphlet for Alpha Aqua and wondering what we might find at the press conference. Brianna wishes she had brought all kinds of gizmos. I wish I had just brought a convincing disguise so I can pretend to be a journalist. I have a badge for the *Wall Street Journal*, which I made especially for the purpose, but it's back on my desk at home. Brianna laughs when I tell her this. The more time I spend with Brianna on her own, the more the CCs seem to fade away.

We reach the Barbican by half nine, the huge concrete complex looming over us. The Barbican is many things – lecture halls, cafés, shops, art gallery, flat blocks – but we're heading for the conservatory, a huge glasshouse filled with tropical plants, cacti and big ponds with koi carp as long as my arm. It's usually only open on a Sunday. Me and Dad used to go there a lot after Mum died, just to get some quiet, bringing packed lunches and eating them under the canopy of creeper vines.

We get the lift up to Level Three with a TV crew carrying cables and tripods. In the hall, journalists are milling around, sipping takeout coffees.

'Follow me.' I grab Brianna's wrist and pull her through the crowds. If we stay still for too long, or look too surprised to be there, someone will spot us. I know the way to the conservatory, but take us the other way. I can see a security guard on the other side of the room, barring entry.

'Where are we going?' Brianna asks.

'I've got an idea.' I say. The idea isn't based on very much. In fact, it's based on just one thing – a smell. There's no café on Level Three, but from somewhere I can smell freshly baked pastries. We weave through the camera crews and reporters and come out on the other side of the crowd, go down the corridor, turn once, and there they are, just like I hoped – three long trestle tables covered with trays. There are people unloading boxes of tiny pastries on to the trays, ready to be served to the guests.

'Oh yum,' is all Brianna manages to say before I pull her on, further down the corridor, out of sight of the catering staff.

'Hey! I was just looking!' she protests.

'I know, but we can't be seen.'

'Do you have a plan?' She's grinning again.

'Sure do. First things first – take off your tie and blazer, and take out your earrings.'

She does as I say, and I do the same. I fold everything up and stash it in a cupboard.

'Let me take a look at you . . .' I check Brianna over from head to foot and do up the top button of her shirt. 'There – you look just like the catering staff now.'

'Eh?' Brianna frowns, looking down at her clothes – black skirt and tan tights, white shirt – then smiles slowly.

'Agatha, you're a *genius*.'

I shrug, enjoying the compliment. 'It's a possibility.'

⌐○

When we get into the centre of the conservatory, the stage has been set up with a lectern bristling with microphones. We're both carrying a tray of pastries on one hand, trying to look like we know what we're doing. After we've seen the caterers leave with the first round of trays, we go over to the tables. Brianna has spotted a couple of spare aprons stashed in a box, and we put them on, completing our disguises. We grab a couple of trays and follow the caterers.

The hall is now empty, with just a bouncer on the door to the conservatory. For a moment, I'm sure he will stop us to ask for our security passes, but we walk confidently towards him and he waves us through. We don't say anything, but Brianna and I exchange a look, and she mouths, *yes!*

We walk on into the conservatory. If the day is warm outside, it's even warmer in here. The air is fuggy and smells of soil. Around us is an oasis of green – palm trees and climbing plants on every side. I want to stay close to Brianna, but if we stay too close it will look strange. We walk through the crowds that have gathered in a clearing in the middle of the conservatory. There's so much to think about, I keep forgetting to stop so people can get a pastry.

'Hey, kid, slow down!' The voice makes me freeze, but it's just a man wanting to get some food.

I survey the scene – a dozen cameras are dotted around, some from the balconies that rise on each side of the room. They peep out between hanging vines and brightly coloured flowers. There are press photographers on the ground, with two rows of chairs taken up by reporters. Each of them has been given a paper bag, with the same bottles of mineral water and the same pamphlet. I read through the pamphlet already, but the language was so vague, I couldn't make out much. There are phrases like 'enabling synergy', 'paradigm shift' and 'holistic approach'. Just jargon.

One phrase stood out for me, though – 'The Face of Tomorrow'.

Before I can think about much else, there is a smattering of applause from the front of the hall, which spreads through the room, as a man in a dark suit steps on to the stage and up to the lectern. His movements are careful and controlled. Over the PA a voice says – 'Please welcome the CEO of Alpha Aqua, Mr Patrick Maxwell!'

I look back to the stage, where Mr Maxwell is waiting for the applause to die down. Most of the cameras are trained on him, while a couple sweep the audience. I can't say why, but I don't like the feel of him. Although not very tall, Maxwell has broad shoulders and a thick neck like a rugby player. His face is angular, framed by a well-trimmed beard. There's a hungry look in his eyes.

'Thank you all,' Maxwell begins. His accent is

measured, middle class and southern. I don't recognise the man, but his voice is strangely familiar.

'I would like to thank the Barbican for allowing us in here today. What beautiful surroundings! I would also like to personally welcome everybody watching this broadcast. I'm here today on behalf of my company, Alpha Aqua, with some news relating to the crisis that has affected us all.'

'Doesn't look like it's affected him much, does it?' whispers Brianna, passing by me again with her tray. I really should be moving around more, offering pastries, but I'm trying to take in everything about Maxwell.

'Of course I don't need to tell any of you about the crisis, which has brought the capital to a standstill – a crisis that shows no sign of abating. You don't have to read the paper or watch the news to know what's happening.'

I look around the room. Everyone is focused on Mr Maxwell. Normally, in a gathering of this size, there would be some whispering, some shuffling and fidgeting. But here, it's as though a very powerful magnet has been placed in the middle of the room.

'So it's with some relief – and great pride,' Maxwell continues, 'that I have come here today to announce a solution to this crisis.' He pauses for effect – murmurings ripple through the crowd. Flashbulbs are going off, but he seems not to notice.

'I am here to announce the future, but I must begin by talking about the past. Two years ago, my company invested in a small laboratory that was pioneering water-purification techniques. With the support of Alpha Aqua since then, the laboratory has been working in secret . . .'

He talks about the purification centre – a giant factory to the north of London. My eyes wander over the crowd, watching their reactions to Maxwell.

'With the advent of this crisis in our own country I authorised a payment of one billion pounds to ramp up production immediately.'

Another pause, and another round of hushed whispers. Someone hands him one of the branded bottles, and he unscrews the lid, slowly takes a sip of the water, and continues.

'Under each of your chairs you will have found

a bag containing an information pack and a bottle of water. A bottle like any other – like the bottles of water that are being fought over, right now, in the street . . . Except there is one difference. All the water in these bottles originated from polluted London water, and was purified in our plant.'

There were mutterings from the reporters, and a few people say 'yuk' under their breath.

'As I speak, Alpha Aqua is producing millions of bottles of fresh water every hour, from our north London plant. Within the week we will begin construction of our own water-pumping system, replacing the corrupted pipes already in existence, to provide fresh Alpha Aqua water to every home in the capital . . . for a reasonable price.'

The room bursts into chatter, and there is another frenzy of flashbulbs. Maxwell smiles thinly. I let the sound from the stage fade into the background. I've found out a lot in a short space of time, and I'm still catching up. The more I focus on the man on the platform, the more uncomfortable I feel. I look around for Brianna. I can see the back of her head, and she is in some kind of heated discussion with one of the catering staff.

Uh-oh. I think. *Time to go*.

⌐○

We get out of the Barbican by the skin of our teeth – ties and jackets in our hands as we run down the stairs to ground level. The head caterer spotted us both as the speech started, but kept quiet to avoid a commotion. In fact, if he hadn't been so worried about his reputation, we'd have been thrown out long before Maxwell had said a word.

Brianna had realised that she couldn't talk her way out of the situation and had dumped the half empty tray on the head caterer, running back through the crowds to the exit, in the direction I was already going. I glanced back for a second, and I could have sworn I saw Maxwell looking over the crowds, right at us, as we hurried out of the room.

'Are you taking those with you?' Brianna laughed. For some reason I hadn't thought to ditch my tray.

'Oh you know – just something for the journey home.'

'More like the police station at this rate,' Brianna quipped, halfway through pulling the apron over her head, still running.

'Oi!' the bouncer shouted as we raced past him.

Back on the street, we look around but found nobody was chasing us. Brianna gasps for breath, her always-perfect hair a mess.

'That. Was. *Awesome.*'

I smile. 'It was pretty fun, wasn't it?'

'Come on, then.'

'Where are we going?'

'Back to St Regis – I don't want to get you into any more trouble.'

'I thought I was the one getting you into trouble?'

'Well, you gave me an adventure – the least I can give you is a good alibi!'

Brianna is as good as her word. When we finally get back to St Regis and are escorted to the headmaster's office, Brianna has a bandage wound round her head (the bandage was in her school bag – I'm starting to admire her more and more).

'And would you two care to explain where *on earth* you've been?' the headmaster begins, his anger disarmed by Brianna's 'injury'.

'Well, sir, we were walking to school together when I tripped over this tree root in the middle of the path and knocked myself unconscious!'

I'm not surprised to discover that Brianna is a pretty good actor – she even manages to make her voice sound shaky, as though she's suffering from concussion.

'Agatha called an ambulance and went with me to A & E.'

The headmaster frowns.

'And why, Miss Oddlow, if you were capable of phoning an ambulance, could you not call the school to let us know where you were?'

I scramble to think of an excuse – mobile phones

are not my field of expertise. Luckily, Brianna chips in.

'She's out of credit.'

This seems to do the trick, though the headmaster still has some doubts about Brianna's injury, eyeing the bandage with suspicion. I think we're rumbled, but Brianna winces in pain and wobbles a little on her feet.

'Both of you go to your next classes,' the headmaster sighs.

We go our separate ways outside the office, with one last grin passing between us. I go back to my lessons and to my own thoughts. It's been an exciting morning, but what have I really learnt? I don't much like Patrick Maxwell, that's for sure, but that's not much to go on. Lessons go by in a haze as I think about everything that's been going on.

Finally, the bell rings for the end of the day and I march away from St Regis, the sky full of red, the air like the inside of an oven. My mouth is parched.

Liam and I haven't spoken all day. We were in different classes, and I hadn't seen him at lunchtime so perhaps he has already gone home. I walk and walk, grateful to be moving. I'm heading back to Hyde Park, but I realise I really don't want to go home – I want to revisit the tunnel under the Serpentine.

I'm impatient to get back to investigating. There's another emotion too – I'm angry with the Gatekeepers' Guild. I was a hapless bystander at the attack on the professor, but that has got me caught up in . . . whatever this is. The Guild brought this danger to my door, but now they won't tell me anything more and they are nowhere to be seen. If they really think my life is in danger, surely they should be around to protect me?

As I march along Upper Brook Street, I become aware of footsteps following close behind me. I walk faster, but they match me. Adrenaline rushes in, and my heart starts to knock against my ribs. Someone is on my tail.

'Agatha, stop!'

I jump – it's Liam. In my relief I feel the tension drain out of me, as if someone has pulled the plug.

'Hey. I thought you'd gone home.'

'No,' he says flatly.

I want to tell him about me and Brianna going to the press conference, and about dressing up as waitresses, but for some reason it doesn't feel like the right moment. I take a deep breath.

'Liam?'

'Yeah?'

'I know that you're annoyed. I get it. And maybe it isn't fair to ask for this, but I really need your help.'

He sighs. 'I dunno, Agatha. Everything is just –' he shrugs – 'crazy right now.'

'I know.'

A smile flickers over his face, then comes back to stay.

'Oh, Agatha – life would be dull if it weren't for you. What is it you want exactly?'

'I want you to come with me to the tunnels,' I say.

⚷

We need supplies to take with us – drinks, food, gas masks, waterproofs – so we head to Groundskeeper's Cottage first.

Dad is still working in the park so we are able to discreetly grab some apple juice from the fridge. Liam pokes around the dead experiments in the kitchen while I go and change into black jeans and a long-sleeved T-shirt. I give Liam the gas mask and find swimming goggles, plus a handkerchief to tie round my mouth. I get us each some waterproof trousers to cover my jeans and his school trousers, and a couple of jackets. I have my own waders, but Liam has to wear Dad's spare pair, which come up past his knees. Protected as well as we can manage, we take torches and trudge from the house, through the heat haze, across the lawns of Hyde Park to the entrance to the tunnel. We look around carefully before we go in. Seeing nobody, I open the gate, and we step into darkness.

It's hard to tell what Liam is thinking, with his face covered by the mask in the near-darkness of the tunnel, but he makes no sign that he wants to turn back, even as the darkness stretches on. My own legs and back are aching. Although the algae in the Serpentine have been dying off, the fumes are still thick underground. We press on. At one point a particularly large gobbet of slime falls from the ceiling in front of us, and Liam grips my arm in panic. He recovers quickly, loosening his grip and forging on. He knows that I only have a handkerchief to protect me from the fumes. We need to hurry.

We come at last to the cavern under the lake. I was almost expecting the iron door to have been bricked up since my meeting with Professor D'Oliveira. What had she said? I had 'stumbled a little too close for comfort'. But it's still there. My breath is ragged. I take the key from my pocket and fit it into the lock with trembling fingers, wondering if the Guild might have changed the lock. But the door still opens smoothly, and together we step into the brightly lit corridor. Liam removes the gas mask, and I can see the wonder in his eyes. He looks at the plush carpet and panelled walls, mouth hanging open.

'I know you said there was a carpet – but I was

just imagining a concrete tunnel. This is something else . . .' He lets out a low whistle.

'I know,' I say. 'Come on – let's get moving.'

We take off our waders and waterproofs, and stash them in the doorway, together with our torches and protective masks. Liam had the foresight to bring our regular shoes in a carrier bag, and we put them on now. All the time I'm listening for the sound of footsteps, but none come. My heart is in my mouth. Although the professor seems to be an ally, what if this is all a trap? What if she warned me off the tunnels, knowing I wouldn't obey her instruction – that I didn't like to be forbidden to do anything?

'Ready?' asks Liam.

I pull a face. 'As I'll ever be.'

We turn down the corridor to the left, though the choice is random – both directions continue further than we can see. We walk for a couple of minutes in silence. Every fifty steps or so there's a door recessed into the wall. We stop at the first few, but they are all locked and unmarked. We try my Guild key, but it doesn't work. My key might let us into the network through the main door, but there are just as many secrets once you're inside. Just when I'm getting frantic that we have nowhere to hide if someone appears, there's a right-hand turn in the tunnel. My good sense of direction – I never need a map to find my way around London – is uncertain underground without landmarks to guide me. Still, I think we are near my house. Perhaps right under it.

It's dark in the new section of tunnel. Liam runs his hand over the wall, and flicks a switch. More lights come on, spreading down the tunnel in a slow wave of light. Down *five* tunnels. Like fingers unfurling on a hand, they stretch out in front of us in five directions, each one signposted – South Bank, St James, Piccadilly, Westminster and Waterloo. Liam laughs nervously. The sound echoes down the tunnels. In front of us is a rack of bicycles, clearly meant for riding through the tunnels.

For a long moment, I don't breathe. 'But . . . this is right under the park. I'm sure of it . . .'

'You can't *cycle* under London . . .' Liam whispers, holding his head, as if he's entered an alternate universe.

233

I'm about to respond, but my attention fixes on one of the bikes in the rack and my heart starts to beat faster. It's an old sit-up-and-beg, light blue, with a battered basket. Unlike the others, it's covered in a fine layer of dust, as though it hasn't been touched in a long time. I know this bike. I have looked at a picture of it every night for the last four years.

'Are you OK?' Liam prods me in the arm.

I swallow hard. 'This bike . . .' I say, 'it was my mum's.'

'You're sure?'

'I'm sure.' I touch the handlebars and a shiver runs down my spine. This is the bike she was riding when she was knocked down and killed. Or so I had been told. But there is no sign of damage to the frame. The paintwork isn't even scratched. And how did it get down here?

'Agatha?'

Tears are running down my cheeks and my hands are shaking. Suddenly, before I can stop him, Liam puts his arms round me and hugs me. I've never been so close to him before. A sob escapes me.

'What does it mean, Liam?'

'I don't know . . . I'm just so sorry.'

He waits until I've stopped crying, then lets go. I'm a little sad – it felt nice, being held by him. I give myself a mental slap. What am I thinking? Danger is making me crazy. I clear my throat. 'Sorry. I've left a wet patch on your top.'

'Don't worry about it.' He smiles kindly.

I wipe my eyes on my sleeve. 'Let's push on, shall we?'

I take the bike from the rack, blow off the dust, test the brakes, and sling one leg over. It's a little on the high side, but I can manage.

'Come on – pick one,' I say to Liam.

'Are you sure? That bike belongs to you, but for me it just feels like stealing.'

'We'll bring it back. You're just borrowing it.'

He picks the smallest of the other bikes, which is still a bit too big for him.

'So, where do you want to go?' I ask.

'What do you mean?'

I point to the tunnels.

'See those signs? South Bank, St James, Piccadilly
. . . Take your pick.'

'Um . . . that one,' he says, pointing.

I put my foot to the pedal, and start to cycle down
the one marked *Westminster*. Liam follows, sitting
half out of the miniature saddle. This tunnel is
concrete, with lights at regular intervals. Unlike the
stinking tunnel under the Serpentine, this one is
clean and dry, wide enough for us to cycle side by
side. We seem to be moving steadily deeper. It's a
relief to be out of the dry heat above ground. Down
here, it's cool and breezy. Liam cycles ahead and I
chase him. When I catch up, we come to a bend in
the tunnel.

'Better turn our lights on.'

I turn my lamp on, relieved that it still works. We
swerve right into an unlit brick tunnel, older than
the first. Cycling on through the dark, we turn down
another tunnel and I can hear water rushing nearby.

'It must be like a patchwork,' I think out loud.
'There are tunnels that were built to service the
sewers, disused bits of the Underground train system,

old bunkers from the Cold War. Whitehall is riddled with tunnels – did you know that? Chambers and tunnels and vaults under the Houses of Parliament. And *they're* connected by a tunnel that runs all the way under Covent Garden to Trafalgar Square! I bet the Guild has access to all of those, and more besides . . .'

Liam grins back at me – clearly he's feeling the same adrenaline rush as me. My head is reeling.

'But surely people know about the tunnels?' he shouts above the water noise.

I raise my voice in reply. 'I reckon only some of them. Probably nobody knows about *all* the tunnels – or all the entrances to them – except maybe the Guild.' I'm only guessing, but it makes sense. There are as many pathways under the streets of London as along them.

We pass into another tunnel, and now I can't see the walls in the dark and our voices echo back at us. I have no idea where we are. In a glint of light we see a flight of stone stairs and dismount to take a look. Up the stairs we come to a metal door, which is locked. I get my Guild key out, and to my surprise it opens it. We push open the door and peer out, into a garden surrounded by tall, grand buildings.

'Grosvenor Square Garden – near the Roosevelt Memorial!' I say, amazed at the direction our underground journey has taken us.

I close the door again before anyone can notice us. Then we go back down the steps to the subterranean world and continue on our journey. The cool air rushes over us as we speed down the tunnels, so pleasant after weeks of sweltering heat. After a few minutes, Liam stops suddenly, and I follow suit.

'Listen,' he says.

We both fall quiet. There is a rumble in the earth, so deep I can feel it in my chest.

'What is that?' Liam asks.

'I think it's an underground train.'

It's strange – we're so deep underground, but the world down here is anything but dead. I feel as though we've stepped inside a living thing – inside the body of London itself. We cycle on, through dark tunnels and lit tunnels, brick tunnels and plastic tunnels,

tunnels that hum and creak with hidden activity, tunnels as quiet as the surface of the moon. A couple of times I think I hear the sound of human movement, and we freeze, but we see nobody.

Finally, we stop in an unlit brick cavern. We can hear a torrent of water flowing close by, though we can't see it.

'It smells dreadful in here,' Liam shouts.

I look up at a hand-painted sign that hangs from chains on the ceiling. It's rotting away, but the word 'Ranelagh' is still clear.

'This must be the Ranelagh sewer,' I shout.

'I've heard of that – it used to flow into the Serpentine, but it was covered over hundreds of years ago by the city.'

Liam takes his torch and points it down. I'm blinded for a second, but my eyes adjust. We're standing near the edge of a precipice. Down below, a red river flows. The sewer, once called the Westbourne, one of the ancient rivers of London, seethes against the rotting brick. Far below the earth, we stare at millions of gallons of flowing red. If there were sulphurous flames and demons pacing in the darkness, it wouldn't seem out of place.

'Wow,' I say dumbly.

'It's . . .' Liam starts, but is also lost for words.

I'm holding a hand over my nose and mouth, wishing we hadn't left our protective gear in the Guild's entrance hall.

'I don't think we should be breathing this in, do you?' I feel exhausted at the prospect of the journey back. 'Shall we go home?'

'Sure.'

We cycle north again, past countless branches in the tunnels. I see signs for Earl's Court, the National Gallery and Buckingham Palace. I still can't believe this is all down here, but with every passing mile, I come to understand how massive the network is. We enter a tunnel that bears the warning sign – *Danger of death by suffocation – this tunnel is unventilated –* but we carry on unharmed. As I see more of the underground network, it begins to seem more alien. We may as well be on another planet, so empty and lonely is this place.

'Stop for a second,' Liam says. 'I think I saw something back there.'

We dismount and walk back to a small side tunnel, mostly taken up by pipes and cables.

'Just there.' Liam points to a gap in the iron pipes. I press my hands to the cold metal. There's a light shining through.

'What is it?'

'I don't know.'

I press my face closer. It's a gap in the tunnel wall, where cables pass into a space beyond. What I see isn't another tunnel, or a brick vault. It isn't even a slimy cavern, but a large room, carpeted and wood-lined. The room is filled with row upon row of filing cabinets, stretching off further than I can see. Between the cabinets, men and women in business dress are moving, looking through cabinets, taking out files, talking to each other.

'It must be a Guild room,' Liam whispers in my ear. 'Looks like they're really old-fashioned about how they store their information.'

I'm speechless. This, more than anything we've

seen, makes my mind reel. There is so much space, so many filing cabinets, each filled with so many files. So much information. But about what? I begin to realise the scale of the Guild, and wonder how my life – and the life of my mother – is tangled up in this huge, intricate web.

'What do you think is in those files?'

'No idea – secret stuff,' Liam says. 'Maybe they've got a file on your mum in there . . .'

He looks for a moment longer, then jumps down and goes back to the bikes. I stay, looking through the gap, watching the men and women as they walk through the maze of cabinets. Hundreds of feet under central London, and nobody outside the Guild knows about any of it.

I want to get into that room, more than anything.

'Come on,' Liam says. 'We ought to go back.'

With a sigh, I go back to my bike. We ride on, down the brick passage. Suddenly there is movement in the tunnel ahead of us, a flash of light. I slam on my brakes, but Liam behind me has no time to react, crashing into my back wheel and sending us both to the floor in a tangle of bike frames. I scramble to get up, but there's no time – the light is coming closer, with the sound of bicycles freewheeling.

We look up to see two men, dressed in plain black, riding a pair of sleek road bikes. They look us over and exchange a confused look.

'How did you get down here?' one of them asks.

'I might ask you gentlemen the same question,' I reply.

The one who hasn't spoken grins.

'Think you're clever, kid?'

'What do want, my grade point average?'

The first one interrupts before he can fire back a witty riposte.

'You'd better come with us.'

⌐○

'Really, Miss Oddlow, I had hoped it would be a bit longer before I saw you again.' Professor D'Oliveira is seated in a green-leather chair behind an enormous desk. It's polished black and gold, with metal sculptures of heads on the legs like figureheads on a ship. I would have reached out to touch the delicate carving if my wrists weren't behind my back in handcuffs. The wood-panelled room is remarkable enough, even if we hadn't reached it by a damp concrete tunnel, deep below Kensington. The *tick tick tick* of an ornate clock behind the professor is the only sound, as I think about my response. I settle for a question –

'Where are we?'

'Isn't it obvious? You were trespassing in Guild tunnels, and now you're in our headquarters.'

We had passed through a cast-iron door that had claimed to be part of the London Sewerage Works, but had, in fact, opened into a hallway area where our captors had locked up the bikes. From there, we had passed into a sort of hall – a wide room with a number of people sitting behind desks. I assumed these were receptionists, and wondered how they all travelled to work in the morning. They couldn't take the number twenty-three bus, that was for certain. Didn't anyone notice these people disappearing under London each day?

We were made to wait as the guards made enquiries

with one of the receptionists, who made a call. Then we were shown down a maze of wood-panelled corridors, into a smaller reception room, and finally into the professor's office.

'Don't you have anything to say for yourselves?' she asks, looking between us. Liam hasn't said a word since we arrived. He isn't the sort of student who gets hauled up in front of the headmaster, and he isn't enjoying being in trouble. 'Not only were you trespassing on Guild land, but you had commandeered Guild property – the bikes.'

'That bike is my mother's,' I say, looking her in the eye. 'So I don't think it counts as Guild property, do you?'

There isn't even a flicker on her face.

'I think these handcuffs are cutting off my circulation . . .' I say at last.

She sighs, then nods to one of the guards who are still standing behind us.

'Remove their restraints. Then you may leave.'

The guard does as he's told and the two of them go. The professor stands. Despite her age – and the stick she leans on – she is a formidable presence.

'Agatha, you have overstepped every boundary today,' she says slowly. 'You will learn what you need to learn, when I am prepared to teach you . . .'

I say nothing for a moment, letting her words sink in. 'So you will teach me one day?' I ask.

Professor D'Oliveira sighs. 'At this rate that day may never come. Today, you have proven yourself insolent, unreliable, reckless . . .'

'I have an important lead in my investigation, though, which I'm trying to follow up,' I say quickly.

The professor frowns and shakes her head. 'What lead?'

'Well,' I say, 'I'll offer you an exchange. If you tell me why my mother's bike – the bike that she was supposed to have been riding when she died – is intact and stored in one of your organisation's bike racks, then I'll tell you my lead.' I sound angry, and I am – how dare they keep secrets from me about Mum?

'I told you that you should *not* be investigating. Why should I let you swan around in our tunnels, endangering the secrecy of the Guild?'

'*Your* tunnels? It seems to me that most of the tunnels you're calling your own actually belong to the London Underground,' I say. 'Or even the London electricity board, or the London sewer system. I'm a taxpayer – or my dad is, at least – so I think I have every right to be in these tunnels, as much as any citizen of Great Britain. Just because you joined up a few of them—'

The professor holds up her hand to silence me, but she doesn't look cross, and, in fact, she just laughs.

'If we've trespassed,' I go on, 'then surely the Guild is trespassing every day! And what are you going to do to us anyway? Hand us in to the police? That wouldn't sound good, would it? 'Dear officer, we caught these two trespassing in our network of secret tunnels that extends across London for our super-private crime-fighting organisation, which is far better than yours – please don't tell anyone. Oh, and we've got the bike here that supposedly one of our agents was riding when she died. It's in surprisingly good shape, considering, isn't it?"

The professor just sits there for a long moment,

clearly taking it all in. I glance at Liam, who is staring at me with his mouth open. I have no idea where this burst of anger came from, but it isn't going away.

'So, seeing as you won't be handing us in to the authorities, would you mind telling us what you know about the water crisis?'

'Why should I tell you anything, Miss Oddlow?' Professor D'Oliveira says, closing the book that has been lying in front of her.

Apparently the interview is over. The professor presses a buzzer and calls an escort of guards to show us out of Guild HQ. We are handed bikes by the guards, each in a dark uniform. Liam is given a plain black bike by the female guard. The man holds out a red mountain bike to me.

'That's not my bike,' I yell at him.

He looks confused. 'I was given this bike for you.'

'Well, I want my own bike, please.' I put my hands on my hips.

'Here in the Guild we take what we're given,' he says.

'How nice for you. Well, I don't. And I want my

own bike back, please. It's light blue with a basket on the handlebars.'

'Is there a problem?' The professor has caught up, leaning on her stick.

'Yes. I want my bike back, please. Mum's bike,' I say.

She smiles for the first time in a while. '*Your* bike? All of the bikes here belong to the Guild.'

I feel panic set in. 'What have you done with my mum's bike? I have so little of hers . . .'

'And what would you say to your father?' she asks. 'How would you explain the reappearance of your mother's bike, after all these years?'

I say nothing. She has a point.

'If we let you have the bike to ride back to the entrance, will you promise to leave it in the rack, where you found it?'

I nod, not trusting my own voice.

'Very good. Please bring Miss Oddlow the blue bike with the basket.' She turns back to me. 'The bike will remain with us, for your sole use.'

'Thank you.'

'Well, go on, then,' she says to the guard.

The guard is staring at me. 'Miss . . . Oddlow?' He looks at the professor as if she'd claimed she could see Father Christmas or the Abominable Snowman.

'Yes, Nelson,' she says impatiently. 'This is Clara's *daughter*, Agatha.'

He turns back to me, mouth open.

'Well – get the bike, then,' says the professor.

'Of course!' He hurries to an anteroom and comes back, a moment later, with the bike. Passing it to me, he whispers, 'Your mother was a legend around here.'

Again, a lump rises in my throat and I can't seem to think of anything to say in reply, so I just nod stiffly. We're shown back out into the tunnel. The guard points along it.

'Up that way, then right at the fork and take the brick tunnel that curves to the left,' he says casually, as though he's giving directions to the corner shop. Then he goes back inside and shuts the door.

We stand there, dumbfounded. Then Liam hugs me for the second time that day. 'What on earth was going on back there? All that stuff about your mum.'

I shrug and release him before getting on the bike and starting to pedal. 'I don't know, but I'm going to find out what really happened to her.'

'We both will.'

Following the directions, we cycle until we reach the end of a tunnel that has no branches, just a cast-iron staircase spiralling up. Liam gets off his bike.

'Look –' he points to the words daubed on the wall of the tunnel – 'Hyde Park. Maybe we should take a look?'

I get off my bike too, and walk the short distance to the staircase. It curves round tightly, as though there was very little space to work with. We climb and climb, so that I'm panting by the time we reach the top. Finally, we come to a small red-painted door. I take the Guild key from my pocket and try it in the lock. The door clicks open, and we step out on to a balcony. Warm air whips around me.

'Where . . .?' says Liam.

'You're kidding,' I whisper in awe.

Beneath us is a carpet of trees, and off on the

horizon I can see the London Eye and the Houses of Parliament. I know this view, but for a moment I can't place it. I look up, over my shoulder, and see a huge bronze angel, wings spread over us.

'We're on the Wellington Arch!'

11.

A VISION OF THE DAMNED

I stand on the top of Wellington Arch for a long time, trying to refocus. There's a light breeze ruffling my hair. It's nice up here – I want to stay. But I have to go down the steps and re-enter the real world of Hyde Park, of heat and dryness and thirst. The tunnels were a distraction. Hiding underground was only delaying the inevitable – I have a job to do.

My mind wanders back to the man who attacked me outside the RGS. He terrified me, plain and simple. I look up again at the sculpture of the Angel of Peace, steering her chariot of war pulled by four stallions. *Courage against adversity*, I think, as Liam and I climb down the stone steps into the park. Whatever needs facing, there is no point in putting it off. I say goodbye to Liam and march home.

As I open the front door, I'm greeted by a pitiful Oliver, draped in what looks – and smells – like dead pondweed. It seems as though he must have got up on to the surface and knocked one of the containers over himself.

'Oliver, you stink! Don't come near me!' I push him away with the toe of my shoe. The last thing I need is slime on my jeans – with the water shortage, washing clothes has become a luxury. 'What have you been doing?'

He mewls and looks up at me with baleful eyes. I crouch, holding him at arm's length so I can study the stuff clinging to him.

I sigh – I really don't want to look at the state of the kitchen. It's bad enough that we can't wash up now we've run out of bottled water. I've been eating all my meals off paper plates. The contents of Dad's rainwater butts are OK for some jobs, but aren't fit for human consumption. I walk towards the kitchen. Through the open door, I can smell familiar fumes – the stench of the algae.

I step further into the room and see the fish tank Dad opened this morning to show me its withered contents. The bag of sugar that Dad keeps on the side – for the three sugars that he stirs into every mug of tea – is upended in the tank. The algae are foaming their way upwards and out of the tank, over the worktop, down the cabinets, and across the floor.

They *squirm*.

Oliver hisses loudly and runs towards the algae as if to challenge them, then mewls again as his paws slide on the damp floor. He races behind me. I take a step back too – it's hard not to feel that this slimy, writhing *thing* wants to hurt us.

'Come on, Oliver.'

I scoop him up and we go through to the living room, where I hold my nose and begrudgingly try to calm him on my lap, but he keeps clawing threads out of my jeans.

'Ow, Oliver – you're hurting me.' I let go and he jumps from my knees, then runs under an armchair. Clearly, he thinks this is my fault and nothing to do with him knocking over the sugar bag. But I'm piecing things together at last. All the foods that Dad tried, from the meat to the vegetable peelings, were missing one ingredient – refined sugar. That had to be the secret power source for the slime clogging London's arteries. But how was it getting into the Ring Main?

I roll up my sleeves and head to the kitchen, throwing open windows and rolling up my jeans. The algae have stopped growing, just frothing a little, air popping like bubble gum on its surface.

Right – say goodnight, slime!

Dad gets home just as I'm putting cheese sandwiches together to toast under the grill.

'What's been going on here?' he asks, kissing me on the cheek and walking over to the now-empty tank.

'Oliver upturned your bag of sugar,' I say casually. 'And it turns out the algae have a really sweet tooth.'

'Sugar?' Dad sits down on a chair. 'I never thought of that.' He seems dazed, but he quickly comes to his senses. 'I need to tell someone – I need to let the authorities know!'

'Yes, you should.'

He looks frantically around the kitchen for the cordless telephone, which is always getting lost. 'Sugar? But how on earth is it getting into the water supply?'

'I don't know.' I don't add the word 'yet', though I'm thinking it. I'm determined to discover exactly what is going on – and to stop it.

The next morning is Tuesday. I wake from another nightmare – red slime, people drowning, dark caverns under the earth. Unlike last time, I don't jump up. The weight of the dream pins me to the bed. My breath is shallow and I'm drenched with sweat. I don't want to open my eyes. How could something so horrible have come from inside my own head? I remember when I used to enjoy my dreams – when they took me away to a case needing solving in a remote country house, or on a train trapped in the Siberian snows. I remember those dreams of old and feel betrayed.

My walk to school is different this morning. There are no rioters, looters or protesters. The streets are as calm as I've ever seen them. The crisis isn't over – tens of thousands of people still don't have running water – but London has been pacified by Maxwell's speech. There are lorries on the road, carrying water through the capital, but now they bear the blue logo of Alpha Aqua. I walk past a huge billboard that shows a bottle of ice-cold water, with 'ALPHA AQUA' in person-high letters.

As though reassured by the words of a doctor – 'You're not better yet, but you soon will be' – the capital has got back into bed to wait for the cure.

Maxwell's cure.

I miss the noise. When there was noise, it was as

if London was crying out for help. But the silence is eerie – in the silence, it feels like there's no hope.

There's no special assembly at school today, though there are more free bottles of Alpha Aqua water being handed out at the door. Some pupils are refusing to take the water, claiming they're having Swiss spring water flown in.

'It sounds disgusting!' says one boy. 'I mean, who wants to drink Chloe Simpkins's recycled wee?'

There is a loud burst of laughter from the kids around him. Chloe is passing by, and I see her turning red. I take her arm and steer her through the crowd.

'Pay no attention,' I tell her. I raise my voice, making sure they hear me – 'Their exclusive spring water is probably filtered through cowpats.'

She smiles wanly as we reach the door to her form room. 'Thanks, Agatha.'

'No worries. See you later.'

I go to my own form room, paying no attention

to the chatter around me. I take out my biology textbook and put it on my desk, pretending to read, to stop anyone bothering me. My mind is going over the details of the last week, trying to find connections between the facts. But those connections are as hidden as the underground network. Remembering the tunnels, I try to think of anything I might have missed.

I'm about to replay our time whizzing through the tunnels when I'm stopped by someone sitting down next to me. I expect it to be Liam, but it's Bernie Sipowicz, holding his little black book and looking shady.

Bernie's father works on the London Stock Exchange, and hopes his son will one day too. But Bernie is more interested in gambling on horse races than the price of crude oil. With the help of 'the little black book', he runs the biggest betting ring in St Regis. If you want to put some money on a football match, a reality TV show or the name of the next royal baby, Bernie is your man.

'Morning, Agatha.' He's small and freckled, and

wears red braces like his father. Sometimes Bernie gets beaten up when someone loses all of their allowance on a boxing match, but most people respect him as a useful public service.

'Hey, Bernie. What's up?'

'Just wondered if you fancied a flutter on the big game?'

He has a way of speaking out of the side of his mouth so that teachers won't spot him talking. On the few occasions when a teacher got suspicious and confiscated the black book, they found it full of tiny, cryptic formulas that they couldn't decipher. Bernie always told them it was for his 'extra maths tutoring'.

'Not for me, Bernie, thanks.'

'Fair enough.' He starts to get up. Suddenly, I grab his arm and pull him back down. A thought is coming together in my head. 'Ouch – what is it?'

Mr Laskey looks up from his newspaper at the noise from Bernie, but disappears behind it again when he sees us both apparently studying a biology textbook.

'Bernie, do you know much about the stock exchange?'

He groans.

'What *don't* I know about the stock exchange? Dad hardly ever shuts up about it.'

'Well, do you know much about Alpha Aqua?'

'The water company? Sure, I guess. It was set up by Patrick Maxwell about fifteen years ago . . .' He frowns, unsure why I'm quizzing him.

'And what sort of things do they invest in?'

'Well, water research, obviously . . . but the company is owned by a consortium that invests in all sorts of other things – computer companies, tinned food, science research . . .'

'They invest in other companies?'

'Sure.'

'And if those other companies do well, Alpha Aqua get their money back? Like making a bet?'

'Yeah, except there are no fixed odds – the more money the company makes, the more money Alpha Aqua make.'

'So, since they invested in water purification, they

must be making a lot of money out of the water crisis?'

'Oh, yeah!' Bernie looks enthusiastic for the first time. 'They hit the jackpot on that one! Every day the crisis goes on, they're making millions of pounds. And when they expand their operation to supply all of London, well, that'll make them *billions*!'

Whether it's a welterweight boxer or a listed company, Bernie always admires a money-maker.

'Thanks, Bern.'

'No sweat. Now, I've gotta be off – things to see, people to do.'

He leaves me to my thoughts. There's something niggling me – right at the back of my mind, but I can't grasp hold of it yet. It's like a shy animal – if I try to catch hold of it too quickly, it will bolt. I have to pretend it isn't there, to let it come closer. I look down at my biology textbook, trying to seem busy so that nobody will distract me. I open the page at random – it's the chapter on blood sugar. My mind elsewhere, I read –

'The level or concentration of sugar in the blood

*is regulated by hormones, including insulin. When
the body is unable to regulate blood-sugar levels, this
is known as diabetes.'*

The bell rings for the end of form time, and my
classmates get up and start to make their way to first
period. It feels like an alarm bell is ringing in my
head.

Unregulated sugar levels.

That's it!

The door slams, bringing me to my senses with a
start. Most people have left the classroom – including
Mr Laskey – but someone is still in the room with
me. As I stand up, there's the sound of a key turning
in the lock. Two of the three CCs – Sarah Rathbone
and Ruth Masters – step away from the door. Sarah,
calm and calculating, Ruth her faithful servant, ready
to beat the snot out of me.

'Hello, Agatha,' Sarah says, smiling thinly.

'What do you want?' I ask. Despite the menace in
their manner, I'm impatient. This is no time for
distraction.

Suddenly, my breath catches.

There are only two CCs in the room, not three. One is missing.

Brianna.

Where is Brianna? She hadn't joined me on the walk to school. Now she isn't here, either.

'What do we want?' Ruth sing-songs, stepping closer.

'You're always asking questions, aren't you, Agatha?' Sarah says. 'Like a child, always asking, *why, why, why?*'

She takes a step closer.

'And that's what we want – to hear no more questions from Agatha Oddball.'

My thoughts are reeling, too fast to understand yet. A single question is flashing in my mind.

'Just *listen* to me – where is Brianna?' I ask.

'There you go again – another question!' says Sarah.

'It's like a disease with her,' Ruth says.

'I hope it's not infectious.' Sarah looks mock-worried.

'Do you know where she is?' I ask again.

Sarah sighs, exasperated. 'I have no idea, Odd Socks. She hasn't been answering her phone all morning. Honestly, she's so touchy – I only posted one silly picture of her!'

I don't hear anything else that she is saying, because I'm running towards the door.

'Hey!' Ruth shouts after me, as I scatter chairs and tables behind me to slow her down. 'We're not done with you yet!'

'Well, I'm done with you,' I say through gritted teeth. I open the door, grabbing the key from the lock and step through. Just as Ruth catches up, I slam the door in her face. The handle turns, but I'm quick with the key. She throws herself against the door with more venom than I thought could come from her willowy frame. I breathe a sigh of relief, but it's no time for self-congratulation. Brianna's wellbeing is more important than me escaping a beating from the CCs.

I do some quick thinking. Form time has ended, so all the school gates will be closed. I don't have time for any of my normal St Regis escape routes.

It's time for Plan Z.

It's first period, so Liam will be in the IT suite. I stride over and knock on the door. 'Liam Lau is wanted urgently in the office,' I tell the teacher, with as much authority as I can muster. Luckily, his IT teacher doesn't know me, so she doesn't know that we're friends.

'You'd better go then, Liam,' she tells him. 'Come and see me later about catching up.'

He looks reluctant as he packs up his belongings and comes to meet me at the door.

'What is it, Agatha?' he asks quietly.

'I think Brianna is in trouble,' I whisper. 'We have to track her down. Are you ready to run?'

For once, he doesn't protest that he will miss maths, or that he has a chemistry test he's been revising for. He seems to understand right away. He nods. I walk over to the opposite wall, take off my shoe and slam the block heel into the glass panel of the fire alarm. It shatters, and bells start ringing.

As the classroom doors start to open and the playground gates unlock automatically, I put on my shoe and we start to run. We make it through the open gates, ignoring angry shouts from the school building,

'Liam Lau! Agatha Oddlow! Come back at once – do you hear me?'

It's Dr Hargrave. I figure he can't hate me much more than he does already, so I have little to lose. Liam, on the other hand, is a model student. I want to say sorry to him, but I'm out of breath, and I have a stabbing pain in my ribs. Liam plays badminton and tennis regularly, and all that running around is coming in handy now. He glances back and realises he's left me behind. He leans against a bus shelter. As I draw level, he joins me, saying,

'Thanks for coming to get me, Agatha.' He smiles.

'I couldn't have all the fun without you.'

'So, where are we going?'

'I'm not sure. Sarah Rathbone said that Brianna hadn't been answering her phone all day, but maybe we should ring it one more time, to make sure.'

'I don't have her number.' Liam shrugs.

'But I do!' I pull out the piece of paper with her address and number that she'd scrawled in the girls' loos. Liam types the number into his phone, presses 'dial', and hands it to me. It starts to ring, and I count three . . . five . . . seven . . . I'm sure it's going to go to voicemail, then someone picks up. I can hear breathing.

'Brianna?' I ask. There is no reply for a moment, just a crackle of static. Then a Glaswegian voice I've heard before speaks.

'Come and get her.'

'Where is she?'

'You're a sweet girl, Agatha. You'll work it out.'

The line goes dead. There's an icy prickle behind my eyes as I pass the phone back to Liam.

'What? Who was it? Where is she?' he asks.

'That was the man who threatened me outside the RGS. He's got Brianna.'

'Why?' he asks, looking at my face.

But I don't answer. I'm thinking hard. There must be a clue in what he said . . . Sweet girl . . . sweet . . . sugar! That's it!

'Liam, can you use your phone to search for anything about Patrick Maxwell and sugar?'

'Sure, hang on . . .' He types furiously on his mobile. A moment later, he hands the screen to me wordlessly. It's a news story from a year before.

> ### SWEET TIMES FOR SUGARKANE
>
> Sugarkane, Britain's third largest sugar manufacturer, today announced a significant expansion to its existing business, made possible by a major new partnership with Alpha Investments. Based in Brixton, the company, which produced 1.1 million tons of refined sugar last year . . .

Suddenly, everything slots together in my mind – all the connections that were hidden under the surface are revealed. I get out my notebook, scribbling down the facts, making sure there's nothing missing –

1. The algae feed on sugar.
2. So both Maxwell's companies – Alpha Aqua and Sugarkane – are making huge amounts of money from the crisis.

3. There is a giant sugar warehouse in Brixton, which has recently expanded its operation - thanks to Patrick Maxwell's investment.

4. Brixton Pumping Station is connected to the underground Ring Main, which carries millions of tons of water around London.

5. Professor D'Oliveira was the target of the hit-and-run - had she found out some of this?

'I think she's at a factory – the Sugarkane factory. It's a company owned by Patrick Maxwell.'

'You mean . . . Maxwell's got her? But why?'

'He's behind all this, I'm sure. And the man who threatened me must be working for him. Brianna was with me at the Alpha Aqua press conference. Maxwell saw us snooping around. They know we're on to them.'

'You went to the press conference with Brianna?' Liam's eyebrow shoots up.

'You weren't talking to me . . .' I start. 'Look, I don't have time to explain now. We need to get to the Sugarkane factory, but I don't want to be spotted.'

'The tunnels, then,' Liam says. 'There's that entry point just down from here, under Grosvenor Square Gardens.'

We jog down the road. Right next to the gate to the garden there is a bike rack, filled with bicycles for hire. These docking stations are placed all over London, part of the mayor's initiative to make cycling more popular.

'Do you have your credit card?' I ask him, pointing to the computer screen next to the bikes. His card is for emergencies only, but I figure this counts.

He nods and selects the option to hire two bikes. We type the codes into the docking station and take the bikes from the racks.

'Where's the entrance?' I ask, my mind going blank for a second.

Liam points to a rhododendron bush a few metres away. 'It was behind that.'

We walk over, wheeling the bikes. He glances around, then sneaks to the back of the huge shrub. There's the metal door we looked through before. I take out my Guild key and fit it into the lock. A click.

Once again, the door swings open easily, the hinges well oiled. Dark steps lead down. Wheeling the bikes, we go in and close the door behind us.

It's very dark at the bottom of the steps, but as we start to pedal, the bicycles' own lights come on, lighting up the way ahead.

We don't speak as we ride through the tunnels. Signposts and patches of rotting algae whizz by. There are signs pointing towards Brixton, Stockwell and Morden, as though it's perfectly normal to travel around London by subterranean passageway. The stale air whips around us, our blazers flapping like capes.

I barely know Brianna, but that doesn't matter – she's a fellow detective, and she needs our help. Creepy images keep playing in my mind like a newsreel – Brianna, bound and gagged in a dim room, a bright light full on her face while Maxwell looms over her, hand poised to strike. Then Maxwell is holding Brianna and sinking her, head-first, into a vat of liquid sugar, laughing and rubbing his hands together. The images are ridiculous – I just wish I could be sure they are wrong.

At least cycling in the cool underground passageways is easier than running in the heat. The going is smooth. We're travelling far faster than any journey above ground could have taken us, through the cramped streets of the ancient capital. From time to time we hear sirens overhead, or the sound of water close by. An occasional rat stops its routine to watch us, not used to humans in this parallel world.

Eventually, one sign points up a staircase to Slade Gardens, which I know is in Brixton. We're almost there. We shoulder our bikes and climb up a metal staircase to the surface.

Brixton is buzzing with activity – the streets are full of people milling around market stalls selling clothes, fish, leather bags, piles of vegetables, cheap sunglasses. There's a band on the corner playing steel drums. Everything is so lively, so jovial, it seems crazy that somewhere nearby Brianna is being held hostage. We cycle on, through the crowds.

Even though it's in London, I had half imagined the Sugarkane factory as a forbidding castle on an island that could only be reached at low tide. Instead, when Liam finally brakes to a halt, we're at the gates of an ugly building, a lump of concrete topped with a corrugated-steel roof. Smoke pumps from funnels, tainting an otherwise clear blue sky. The factory is surrounded by a high fence.

We walk round the perimeter, looking for a chink in the armour. But there are no gaps, and a line of barbed wire coils along the top of the fence.

'It's fairly uninviting.' Liam points to a plaque on the gate, which reads – *Stop! Visitors by appointment only. Trespassers will be dealt with SEVERELY.*

I rummage in my satchel and pull out my lock-picking kit. 'I guess it will have to be a breaking-and-entering job then.'

'Can you do that?' He sounds impressed.

'I dunno. Mum taught me, but it only works on simple locks. Still, it's worth a shot.'

I struggle with the lock for a few minutes while Liam looks on. The lock is much more complex than any that Mum had taught me to crack, but I'm determined not to give in.

'Aggie, I don't think it's working,' Liam says, at last.

I put the kit away, admitting defeat. 'So how are we going to get in, then?'

But even as I speak there's a buzzing sound, and the heavy gates swing open. We look at each other, freaked. There's nobody in the courtyard in front of the factory, and I can't see anyone at any of the windows. I glance up at the camera next to the gate, and it seems to go dark, like an eye closing.

'Do we go in?' he asks in a whisper.

'I have to,' I tell him. 'Brianna might be in real danger, and nobody else knows she's here. You don't have to come, though. It might be a good idea to have someone on the outside, who knows where I am.'

'If you're going in, I'm coming with you,' Liam says.

I smile and nod to him, and we step through the iron gates. The gates buzz again as they shut behind us. We've made it inside. But we're trapped.

12.

THE WHITE MAZE

We stand for a moment, the closed gates at our back, wary of walking further into the grounds.

'We have no choice,' I say at last. 'We have to find Brianna.'

We move through the courtyard at the front of the factory, glancing around for anyone who might be coming for us. But there's not a soul in sight. It's eerie, knowing that someone saw us through that camera and opened the gates. But it's too late to turn back now.

We creep down the side of the main building until we reach a pair of huge wooden doors, which are three times my height and wide enough to take a lorry.

I slowly push one of the doors open, keeping to the side in case someone is waiting to grab us. The door is heavy, and I have to put all my weight into pushing it. Nobody appears, and it's dark inside. I look at Liam, who seems more uncertain by the minute.

'Come on,' I say, and step into the dark.

He follows, and closes the door behind us. We're in some kind of loading bay, and the air vibrates with a low hum. It feels like we've stepped into a buzzing hive. We stay still for a long moment, making no noise, hoping nobody has heard us enter. When nothing changes, I tug Liam's sleeve and we edge through the darkness. At the other end of the bay I can see a sliver of light. It's coming through the side of a door that has no lock. I look through the crack at the side of the door and see a vast room, full of what looks like stacked sugar cubes. But they aren't sugar cubes – they're sugar crates, painted white. The room is enormous.

I move to one side to let Liam have a look.

'What is it?' he whispers.

'This must be where they store the sugar. I think we're in the warehouse.'

He looks through the gap. 'There must be a million crates in there . . .'

'Can I have another look?'

I press my eye to the door again, searching for anything that might help us. The white crates are piled as high as a double-decker bus, and ahead of us is a path between them. I can see nothing to our left or right. The only way is forward. On the ground, a coloured spot against the white – a blue jacket. My heart thumps.

The jacket is Brianna's – the one she wore over her uniform instead of her blazer, and I point it out to Liam.

'What now?' Liam whispers. 'How are we going to move without being seen?'

'Once we're among the crates, I don't think anyone will be able to see us. I can't see anyone at the moment . . . Let's go.'

Liam grabs my arm to hold me back. 'And what if someone *does* see us?'

'You've got legs, haven't you?'

'Since when did you turn into an action hero, Agatha?'

'When it became the only option . . . Come on.'

I shake his hand from my arm, and push the door back. I step into the room and Liam follows. The door swings shut behind us, and we each put up a hand to shield our eyes. The fluorescent light shining off the crates is dazzling. For a moment, I can do nothing but wait for my eyes to adjust to the glare. Once I can see clearly, I start along the path, with Liam close behind me. Though we try to move silently, our footsteps echo in the huge space.

We walk down an avenue of sugar crates. They're piled high on either side, towering above our heads – I suppose these paths are left for forklift trucks to get through the stacks. We pass avenues branching off in both directions. We're in a gigantic maze. The air is musty-sweet with sugar dust. All the time Brianna is in my head, and I feel I should be running instead of creeping. I fight the urge – if we get lost in the labyrinth, we can't help her. As we walk, I make a mental note of how many turnings we pass on each side. Suddenly, from above us, a booming voice echoes –

'Nice of you to join us, Miss Oddlow–low–low!'

Liam says nothing, but he's turned pale. I recognise the Glaswegian accent from before.

'Come on,' I say to Liam. 'Don't let him scare you.'

I point to the ceiling, where CCTV cameras are fixed every few metres.

'He knows we're here, but I don't think he's in this room.' I sound more confident than I feel.

We turn left and right, down paths that widen and narrow. I mutter as I count the turnings under my breath. Some are a dead end, others split off to countless smaller paths. In some places, the white crates aren't stacked straight up, but overlap like steps. We walk and walk – and soon, despite my attempt to keep track, I feel my head spinning in this alien landscape. The voice over the speakers booms out again –

'And you brought a friend—end—end!'

This time, the accent is polished and southern – a public schoolboy's voice. This is definitely Patrick Maxwell – the suave figurehead of Alpha Aqua.

'Do you have any idea where we're going?' Liam asks.

'No, but I feel like we're going round in circles . . . I'm going to climb that hill and have a look around.'

'Hill?'

'OK, stack of crates. Don't you feel like you're in a snowy valley?'

'Yeah . . . It's creepy, isn't it? Are you sure it's safe to climb up there? What if someone sees you?'

'Well, it's not like they can get to us quickly. Stay here.'

I climb on to the first crate, then another and another. By the time I've climbed fourteen steps, Liam is far below. My breath is ragged from the climb and the fear of falling. Gripping the crate in front of me, I turn to look. The view makes me dizzy. In all directions are white hills and valleys, a wintery landscape. Below me I can see the paths, branching off in all directions, as far as the eye can see. What lunatic made this? Certainly, no warehouse foreman in his right mind – it's like the work of an obsessive giant, stacking the contents of his sugar bowl.

I imagine that I'm holding a polaroid camera in my hand. I hold it up to the maze and take a picture. The camera clicks and a little photo slowly scrolls out of the slot. I wait for a moment, while the memory-photo develops – turning from black to snowy white. I look at it closely, studying the paths. One part of the maze catches my attention. A single path leads to a clearing. I can't see what's in there, but it's roughly in the middle of this gigantic room. I start to climb back down to Liam.

'Follow me,' I tell him.

'Where?'

'I'm not sure, but I have a theory.'

We walk on through the maze and Liam keeps quiet, sensing that I need to concentrate. If I think about anything else for a moment, the photograph might fade. Once or twice, I think I hear footsteps that aren't our own, but it might just be an echo.

Every time I give a signal to stop, there's total silence. We walk on, and I know we are close to the clearing. I pause for a second at a junction, trying to see from the picture what happens next. If Liam thinks it's weird that I'm staring at a patch of blank air above my hand, he doesn't say anything.

The stacks of crates around us are sheer – there's no way to climb up and look. I choose at random, turning left. We walk a short way, turn left again, and we're in the clearing. It's a perfect circle, stepped as though ready for an audience. It reminds me of old Roman amphitheatres, where Christians were thrown to the lions as entertainment.

And there in the middle of the floor, tied up on her side, is Brianna.

'Brianna!'

Her eyes open wide. I run to her. She can't speak – there's tape over her mouth, and her whole body has been trussed up in a knot of ropes. She makes grunting noises, rolling her eyes, trying to communicate. I try to undo the ropes, but can't find a start or finish to them. Liam steps in.

'Let me.'

I stand back and watch this new cool-in-a-crisis Liam. He untangles a few of the knots and the rest fall away. Brianna sits up and tears the tape from her mouth, gasping the sugar-filled air.

'You came for me . . .' She looks close to tears.

'Brianna!' I can't resist hugging her. 'How did you get here?'

'I was just stepping out of my front door when someone put a bag over my head! They must have sedated me, because next thing I knew, I was here.' She pauses to adjust her hair. 'Uh, speaking of which, where *are* we?'

'We're in a sugar factory in Brixton,' Liam says.

'Oh right, of course.' Brianna smirks. 'Makes perfect sense. So how did you find me?'

'Just used my little grey cells.' I smile as I catch Liam's eye.

'Yes, you're a little too good at that, aren't you?' a voice says behind us.

I spin round to see Patrick Maxwell step into the clearing, his dark suit contrasting with the maze like an old black-and-white film. Calmly, he reaches inside his jacket and takes out a gun. With the appearance of that little piece of metal, I feel my heart begin to pump hard as adrenaline rushes into my system.

'Do you like my labyrinth? It's great for hunting parties. You can set your prey loose and, however fast they run, they don't stand a chance.' This time his voice is posh again, jocular – and I realise this time whose voice it is – it's the voice of Davenport, the man who said he was from the Environment Agency, who visited Dad.

'I'm afraid it's game over, little girl,' he says. But this time he says it in a different voice – another voice I know – with a thick Glaswegian accent.

And suddenly I make the connection – the man outside the RGS, Davenport, Patrick Maxwell – they are all the same person. And that person is completely *nutso*.

The three of us – Brianna, Liam and I – step closer together, huddled in silence. Brianna seems shaky, and Liam and I have to support her between us.

Maxwell starts to chuckle as he watches us. It starts as nothing more than a giggle, then builds to rolling, crazed laughter.

'It was just a daydream I had one day,' Maxwell goes on in a different voice – the drawl of the Deep South of America this time. He might be crazy, but I have to admire his impressions. 'I sure am impulsive like that. But that's the nice thing about havin' money and power over people, ain't it? You can do whatever you darn well please.' He smiles thinly and goes back to his Scottish accent: 'But you, Agatha Oddlow – I can't control you; you've made that much clear. And there's only one future for people I cannot control.'

He cocks the gun.

'Whoa!' Brianna screams, her voice strangled. 'Put the gun down.'

I know I should be thinking of a way out, but I can't take my eyes off the gun.

THiRD-GENERATiON
Smith & Wesson
Pearl-Handled
Floral Scrollwork on the Barrel
PROBABLY MADE AROUND 1935

It's an expensive gun – elegant, even beautiful to look at. But that won't make much difference when it blows the little grey cells out of my skull.

Liam's hand reaches round Brianna to take mine, and I don't shrug it away.

'Stand where I tell you, the three of you,' Maxwell says, gesturing with the gun. 'You on the left, Miss Pike –' he points to Brianna – 'then Mr Lau in the middle. I look forward to shooting you last, Miss Oddlow.' He smiles brightly, as though he's handing out presents.

With little choice, we do as he says, and for a moment he lets the silver revolver drop to his side, knowing that he has us where he wants us.

'Don't you just look delightful? I wish I could take a picture . . .'

Maxwell is grinning evilly, and is raising the gun again when Liam lets go of my hand. He dashes forward, taking Maxwell by surprise, and barrels head-first into his stomach. Maxwell is knocked on to his back, winded. The gun flies from his hand.

'Run!' Liam yells, scrambling to his feet.

He doesn't need to tell us twice. Brianna has recovered quickly from her ordeal and is already at the edge of the clearing, where she stoops to pick up the fallen gun. I follow close behind, with Liam at my elbow. Maxwell must have had a second gun in his pocket, because a moment later, two shots whizz past my ear, striking the crates in front of us. They burst with a cascade of sugar. We skid on the slippery granules, but keep running. We race round the corner, out of his line of fire, but there's no time to waste – I can hear Maxwell staggering to his feet.

'You can't escape!' he calls after us, but the confident tone in his voice has gone.

We run through the maze, left and right, far too quickly for me to get my bearings. We start running down a long path, with no branches at all. At the end of the path, I can see an ordinary brick wall – the edge of the maze! But it is so far away. If Maxwell catches us in this corridor, we'll be sitting ducks for his gun.

'Stop!' I yell.

The other two skid to a halt. I can hear him getting closer.

'What are you doing?' says Brianna. 'He'll be here any minute!'

'Exactly – we can't let him catch us. Give me the gun.'

'What?' Liam yelps. 'Agatha, you're not a *killer* . . .'

'Just give it to me!'

Brianna places the gun in my hand. It's cold and heavy. I've never held a gun before, but I have read enough about them to know how to fire one. The footsteps are so close . . .

'Get back!' I shout to Liam and Brianna. I put both hands on the gun, take aim at the bottom crate in the nearest stack, and fire.

The first shot knocks me back like a punch in the chest, but I aim again and keep firing at the crate. Sugar spills everywhere, and the wood splinters. Finally, I'm still pumping the trigger, but there are only dull clicks – I'm out of bullets. For one awful moment, I think I have miscalculated. But now the smashed-up crate starts to creak and groan. It's right at the bottom of the giant stack, the white cliff towering above me. The box cracks, splinters flying, and now the stack is starting to lean.

Just before I turn, Maxwell rounds the corner and takes aim. I run, and behind me there is a crash like rolling thunder. Looking over my shoulder, I see the white cliffs collapsing like a landslide, smashing crates to smithereens. A sugar-powder cloud billows down the empty canyon, faster than I can run, wrapping me in choking sweetness. I run on, coughing and half blind, until I reach the end of the path, where Liam and Brianna are waiting for me.

'Agatha – are you OK?'

'I think so.' I'm still spluttering, but we're out of

the worst of the sugar dust. My arm aches from firing the gun. I look myself over – ghostly white, covered head to toe in powdered sugar. Looking back into the maze, I can see the wreckage I caused and the sugary mushroom cloud spreading over the room.

'That . . .' says Liam breathlessly, 'was really cool.'

I smile at him.

'What you did back there was so brave. You could have got yourself killed!' I say.

'Don't remind me – I think I might pass out.' He grins. 'Do you think he's . . .?'

'We won't be seeing him for a while anyway. But there's no time to waste – we need to get out of here.'

I look around. We've reached the edge of the maze, but we're not back where we started. We have ended up on the other side of the room, deeper inside Maxwell's lair. In front of us is a lift door.

'Seems like the only option . . .' Brianna says.

'Come on, then.'

I press the call button. We hold our breath, waiting

to see if any alarms go off. None do, and after a moment the doors slide open. We step into the empty lift, and I look at the buttons. There are none going up to higher floors, only '0' and '-1'. Since we are on the ground floor, I press '-1'. The doors close, and the lift starts its descent.

None of us speak, but I can tell from their faces that we're all thinking the same thing. We're hoping that, when the lift stops and the doors open, we won't be met by more guns. After a minute, I realise we aren't going down just one floor – the lift is moving fast, and shows no sign of slowing. For a sickening moment, I think the lift is a trap – speeding faster and faster until we will be smashed to pieces at the bottom of the shaft. But, finally, the rate of descent slows, and we come to a gentle stop. I hear Liam take a deep breath, then the doors slide open once more.

'What the . . .?' Brianna trails off.

'Where are we?' Liam asks.

After the dazzling white of the sugar maze, it takes my eyes a moment to adjust to the darkness. When they do, I can't believe the size of the room we are in. Hewn from the London bedrock is a cavern. In front of us, excavated from its burial like a strange coffin, is a gigantic concrete pipe.

The London Ring Main.

Coming down from the ceiling of the cavern is a complicated array of pipes and taps, ending in a silver pipe, that pierces the Ring Main like a needle. This is it! All the proof I need that my suspicions were correct.

'What is all this?' Brianna asks.

'That –' I point to the pipework above us – 'is where the algae have been coming from. That's where it gets its food – pure sugar, pumped into the water supply . . .'

I am waiting for her admiring response, when a hand clasps a rag over my mouth. In shock, I breathe in, and my nostrils are filled with a sickly-sweet petrol smell – chloroform. The room starts to spin and the sounds around me become distant, as if coming from the bottom of a long corridor. I try to hold my breath, but the grip on me is tight, and I need to breathe in again. A familiar Glaswegian accent speaks in my ear –

'Don't struggle, or I'll break your neck.'

And the darkness takes me.

13.

WHERE NO ONE CAN HEAR YOU SCREAM

When I come to, I'm propped upright, against some kind of pillar – a metal pipe? It takes me a moment to remember Maxwell and the chloroformed rag. The cold at my back is spreading through my blazer and through my veins. I can hear Maxwell's voice nearby, giving orders.

'You two, get your backs against the pipe there. Keep your hands where I can see them. Don't think I won't use this.' As he says this, I hear the sound of a gun being cocked.

Pretending to still be unconscious, I peek through one eye and see Maxwell take two pairs of handcuffs from his belt. His dark suit has turned hazy white with powdered sugar, and his hair and face are ghostly. He sets about cuffing Liam and Brianna to either side of a metal post that supports the Ring Main. They put up no resistance. This isn't like the sugar maze – there's nowhere to run and hide in this huge, empty room. This is a room that nobody in the outside world knows about, where nobody will ever find us.

While Maxwell is securing Liam and Brianna, footsteps approach me from behind. I close my eyes tightly.

'Hello, how did you get down here?' It's a man's voice – one of Maxwell's lackeys. 'Oh, she's sleeping!' he says, poking me with the toe of his shoe.

'Thank you for that brilliant observation,' Maxwell snaps at him.

'Sorry, sir . . . I just mean, they're not supposed to be down here, are they? *He* wouldn't be pleased about that, sir.'

Who is he talking about? I hold my breath, hoping for more information, but all Maxwell says is –

'Well then we better make sure that he never finds out. Understand?'

'Yes, sir . . . absolutely . . . but, well, they're just *kids*.'

'Do you think he cares about that?' Maxwell snarls.

'No, sir, of course, sir.'

I continue to pretend to be asleep. I wish I could stop my hands trembling, which I'm sure will give me away. I struggle to keep still against the mixture of fear and cold. I keep seeing an image of my body lying on the ground in this cavern, rotting away in the dark under London. I imagine Dad looking for me for the rest of his life, never knowing the truth.

'She's sedated, but it'll wear off soon,' says Maxwell in a more jovial tone. 'Tie her up while I deal with these two. The ropes are over there.'

I squint to see what he's doing – he is crouched on the ground, going through Liam's and Brianna's pockets, removing mobile phones, flick-knives and anything else that might help us get out of here. The lackey comes towards me with a coil of rope. I shut my eyes again, frantically trying to think of something clever to do, but the chloroform is still making my brain fuzzy. All I feel is building nausea. I try to swallow down the bile – if I'm sick, it will be hard to pretend to be unconscious.

But then, if I'm sick, it might get me the moment's distraction I need. He stands over me, nudging me again with the toe of his boot. Now he is crouched in front of me, wrapping the rope round the pipe and my wrists. I retch, depositing my breakfast down his shirt.

'You stupid little . . .'

He stands up reflexively, trying to get away from the vomit, and that's when I make my move, kicking out with both legs, knocking him off balance. He falls, crying out and hitting his head on the concrete. He lies there, groaning. One down . . .

Maxwell, his attention caught by the noise, stops what he was doing and comes running.

'What happened?'

I close my eyes again and lie perfectly still. If I can trick him into believing that I'm still asleep, that the vomiting was just a reflex, he might not kill me straight away. It works – he strides over, takes one dismissive look at me, then crouches beside the man, who seems unable to answer him.

'Get up, you idiot.'

The gun hangs in his hand, just out of my reach.

I jump up with all my strength, smashing into the side of Maxwell, knocking him off balance. The weapon slides from his grasp, landing somewhere in the shadows beneath the Ring Main. He hits the floor hard. Luckily for me, he cushions my fall as I land on top of him.

I scramble off him and begin to crawl towards the gun, but he recovers quickly. Just as I reach the gun, his hand closes round my right ankle and he pulls hard. I fall flat on the concrete floor and lie on my stomach for a second, useless and winded. Then I hear Brianna and Liam shouting. I can't hear what they're saying, but they spur me on. I kick out and must catch him full in the face, because he roars with anger.

I crawl forward quickly and grab the gun handle. It feels cold and heavy, like the weapon of destruction it is. I stand up and spin to face Maxwell, who is still on the ground. I'm trembling, so I close my second hand round the first to steady my aim. I point the gun down at my tormentor. He laughs – not the response I was hoping for.

'Careful with that thing,' he says, goading me. 'You wouldn't want to do something you'd regret later.'

My world is spinning; my hands are trembling so hard I can barely hold the gun up.

'I'm not sure I would regret it,' I say, but the words sound ridiculous. I look to Liam and Brianna, but they have gone silent, staring at me. None of us know what to do next.

'Go on then, Agatha Oddlow – shoot me,' Maxwell drawls in his Deep South accent. 'What are you waitin' for? If you're gonna shoot me, do it. You only have to pull that little trigger.'

He's right, of course – I'm never going to shoot him. But if I put the gun down, he wins. There has to be a third way . . .

Oh.

As the thought hits me, I try not to show it on my face.

'Not got the guts for it, eh?' Maxwell says, starting to get to his feet.

'Maybe not, Mr Maxwell,' I say. 'But there's more than one way to skin a cat.'

He pauses, unnerved by my sudden composure.

'Though why anyone would want to skin a cat . . .' I mumble. I turn, aiming the gun at the little pipe that's carrying sugar into the Ring Main and feeding the algae.

I fire – once, twice, three times. The impact from the gun knocks me back at the same moment that Maxwell cries out, realising what my plan is. He springs in front of me and wrestles the gun from my hand.

But he's too late – at least one of the bullets has punctured the sugar inlet pipe high above our heads. Liquid sugar starts to rain down on us. Maxwell makes a grab for me, but I leap to the side and he slips in the pool of syrup and falls. I scramble away, back towards Liam and Brianna, who are calling to me.

The key is still in the handcuffs behind Liam's back. My hands are sticky with sugar and I fumble for a moment – but at last I manage to unlock his cuffs and he takes the key from me and releases Brianna.

From above, there is an ominous ripping sound. Maxwell has run over to a pipe with a huge valve wheel, that he is trying to turn to shut off the flow of sugar. It won't budge. I look up to where the ruptured pipe is leaking syrup – the sheer force of it is tearing a bigger and bigger hole in the main pipe with every second. Suddenly, it gives way altogether, in an explosion of syrup that hits us like a wave.

'Ugh!' Brianna cries, wiping syrup from her face, a bedraggled version of her former self.

After the initial flood, we can see the damage that the explosion has done. Now it's not just the sugar pipe that has a hole – there is a huge hole in the Ring Main too. And, instead of liquid sugar, there is a lava stream of red slime spewing on to the cavern floor. My nostrils fill with the familiar stench as the algae give off their trademark fumes.

'We need to get out of here!' shouts Liam.

The three of us start to run towards the lift door,

as a wave of red slime washes over our feet. But this time Maxwell is ahead of us, wading to the lift and pressing the button. The lackey limps in behind him, just in the nick of time, but we are too late. The doors slide closed as we get there, and the last thing I see is Maxwell, grinning hatefully back at me.

'What are we going to do?' Brianna says, choking.

'We have to get away from the fumes,' I say, but my voice sounds far off. I can't focus – my head is full of fog. The cavern is fast filling up with slime.

'There are some stairs over there!' Liam shouts above the roar of the waterfall. Sure enough, carved into the rock face, there is a door with a window in it, and a spiral of metal stairs is just visible beyond. But the floor is flooding quickly, and the door is already half submerged.

'We have to move fast,' I say, coughing. We start to wade through the foul slime. A couple of times I stumble, accidentally plunging my battered hands into the stinging poison. Liam puts an arm round my shoulders to support me. By the time we reach the door, the algae are up to our chests, and only about thirty centimetres of the door is still visible. Luckily, the door opens outwards. Brianna gets there first and pushes it open, and we half swim through the opening. Liam drags me behind him, until finally my foot is on the first stair.

We start to climb, our clothes heavy with the ooze. My head is buzzing. After being drugged with the chloroform, my fight with Maxwell, and now breathing the fumes, there isn't much energy left in me. Adrenaline can only get you so far, and mine is fast running out. My legs feel wobbly as I climb.

'Come on, don't slow down!' Liam says. He's following me up the stairs, watching my faltering steps.

I look down and can see the red slime rising quickly in the narrow stairwell. As I drag my feet up each stair, one by one, the tide is lapping just below my shoes. Liam scrambles up alongside me, unwilling to go past me.

'It can't be far now,' Brianna says, somewhere above.

I have the sudden feeling that the staircase will

never end – we'll be climbing forever. At this thought, my legs collapse under me, and I fall forward on to the steps. I can hear Liam's voice calling my name, but darkness rises inside me, and I can't move or respond. As I lie here, I can feel the cold slime rising over my legs, up to my waist, my chest . . .

And now I feel . . . nothing.

14.

TRAPPED

White light.

I am a mind without a body, floating in light. Can you float without a body? I don't know. But I have no legs to stretch, no fingers to flex, no eyes to blink. But I am somewhere – I exist. It's peaceful here, and there's no reason for me to want anything to change. If I had lungs, I would let out a long, contented sigh.

I sink back into nothingness.

⌐○

'Hello, love.'

A familiar voice – Dad's. He strokes my hair, then takes my head in both his hands.

'I'm just going to pop out and get myself a coffee. I'll be back soon. I'm so proud of you.'

He kisses me on the forehead, and I sink back into sleep.

'Hello, Miss Oddlow.'

I know this voice. It's the voice of a man with many voices, though this one is perhaps his scariest.

I hear the beeping of a heart monitor in the background, and I hear it speed up. It is my heart.

'Don't worry about moving – I know you can't anyway. Temporary paralysis, the doctor called it.'

Yes, I know this voice – it has threatened me before, and it is threatening me again now.

Patrick Maxwell.

'Big words, but all it means is that you can't run

away. And, judging by that heart monitor, it seems you can hear me just fine.'

I try to control my fear, but my heart keeps racing. I hear the sound of a plastic chair being dragged close to my bed.

'How does it feel, Miss Oddlow, to be trapped in your own body?'

His voice is close now, and I can smell his sour breath. To a passerby he might look like a caring relative, begging me to open my eyes, to wake up, to be all right. He snarls each syllable.

'If you'd had your way, Miss Oddlow, I'd have been caught by now. But you couldn't quite see it through, could you? Still, my career is over. I'll never work in this city again. He'll see to that – he doesn't like people who fail . . .'

He's practically whispering into my ear now. *Who is he talking about?*

I want to ask, but I can't.

'So, we both know what it feels like to be trapped, Miss Oddlow. Except the difference is I'm going to escape this trap you've set for me – I have a private jet waiting to take me away. But you, Agatha – you're going to stay trapped forever. You're never going to wake up. Just like your mum never did.'

Mum? Did he have something to do with that? I hear him lean over and pull something closer, something on wheels. A second later, there's a sharp pain in the crook of my arm.

'They put this needle in you so you could get some water, Agatha. Ironic, really, after all that's happened – it'll be the last drink you ever have. By the time I'm on my plane, you'll be growing cold in the mortuary, and the doctors and nurses will be fighting over who gave you too much pain medication, so that you just stopped breathing, just slipped away . . .'

My heartbeat is racing so fast on the monitor it seems like it will burst right out of my chest. But then the sound stops – the monitor is off. I hear him fiddling with the stand that holds my drip, tampering with the plastic bag. Finally, he sits down.

'There. It's done,' he says, whispering into my ear. 'Goodnight, Agatha.'

I hear him take something from my bedside table, then the sound of water pouring from a jug.

'Here's a toast,' he says, louder now, 'to the late, great detective, Agatha Oddlow.'

I wait, my heart racing away in silence, my fear contained, trapped. I start to feel drowsy again, but still I wait, until –

The door bursts open and two policemen rush in, grabbing Maxwell and forcing him to the floor. I open my eyes and rip the needle from my arm.

'What the . . .!' Maxwell yells in rage.

'Hello, Mr Maxwell,' I say, swinging my legs out of bed. 'In answer to your question I woke about an hour ago. I thought you might come looking for me here, so I had a word with these nice policemen.'

He's breathing heavily, grunting almost, jaw clenched. They put handcuffs on him, and for once Maxwell seems lost for words, in any of his voices.

'Oh, and thank you for speaking clearly,' I say, pulling a small microphone from under my pillow. 'I'm sure your confession will come in handy.'

'You little . . .' he yells, trying to throw the police off and failing. And at last I get to say the words I'd always dreamed of saying . . .'

'Take him away.'

15.

EPILOGUE

'Clean shirt – check. Clean, mended skirt – check. Polished shoes – check. Clean tights – check. Brushed beret and blazer – check . . .'

I tick the items off on my list, feeling with each one that I'm being restored to my former self. I look myself over in the mirror, and my outfit is immaculate. The first hot shower was bliss, and Dad had to tell me to get out after twenty minutes.

It took the water board another week to clean the clogged mains pipes, and it will be another month before everything is back to normal, but the supply to our cottage is back with cool, clear water running from the taps. All over London the red algae have died off without sugar to keep them alive. Tons of dead sludge was dredged from the Serpentine and flushed into the sewers. The broken shop windows from the raids are being fixed, and London is being put back together.

For me, as well, it's time to get back to ordinary life. There's one more day of term to get through before the summer holidays. The last couple of weeks have been terrifying and exhilarating – the worst and best moments of my life. While I'm glad that the threat has passed, I'm also sad that the adventure is over. But St Regis beckons, and – for the time being – I'm still a schoolgirl.

'Morning, Agatha!' JP calls from his bench as I approach on my way to school.

'Morning, JP.'

'Oh, hang on a minute. I wanted to talk to you about something . . .'

As I watch, he takes a familiar object from the inside pocket of his jacket. The red notebook! I haven't seen JP for a few days, and with everything that has happened I'd almost forgotten my suspicions of him spying on us. Without changing my expression, I say –

'Oh, yeah?'

'Well, it might be nothing, but I saw this guy creeping around outside your house the other night. It seemed like he was planning to break in, but then he knocked on the door and spoke to your dad . . .'

'And you were watching the whole time?'

JP shrugs. 'It's not like I've got much else to do. Anyway, it all seemed innocent, but then you'll never guess what happened next . . .'

'I might, actually,' I mutter.

'He disappeared for a while, but later, at about two in the morning . . .'

I listen to JP's story of how the mystery man – Davenport, AKA Patrick Maxwell – had reappeared outside our house in the dead of night, only to chop all the flowers off the clematis plant on the back wall.

He hands the notebook to show me the times he had noted down. When he talks again, the words tumble out super-fast with nerves.

'Seemed like a total nutter to me, but your dad seemed to know him, so I thought, well, it might be a joke between the two of them. But what kind of joke is that? Cutting all the flowers off your friend's plant! So, I wasn't sure what to do. And I didn't want to annoy your dad by admitting to spying on his friend, because maybe he would kick me out of the park . . .'

He's wringing his hands with worry. I hand the notebook back to him.

'You did the right thing, JP – thanks for letting me know.'

He pauses, then his frown lightens to a smile.

'Oh, OK . . . well, good!' The tension melts out of his shoulders. 'You're looking better today.'

'You too, JP.' It's true – he's fresh-faced and bright.

'Well, I've been helping out at one of the local soup kitchens. A woman who works there with me knows the owner of a chain of restaurants, and she's recommended me to them. I've got an interview for a job tomorrow.'

'That's great!'

He nods and grins. 'And your dad said I can use the shower and borrow a suit.'

I laugh. 'Have you seen Dad's suits? He's had them since the Dark Ages. I'm pretty sure they all have huge lapels and brown checks.'

He smiles. 'Sounds like your dad was quite the dandy.'

'That's one way of putting it.'

I fish in my pocket and pull out a sandwich.

'I did like the egg roll you made me the other day,' he says, eyeing the sandwich with thinly disguised suspicion. 'Have you started experimenting again?'

'It's only Marmite with peanut butter. I thought the protein and vitamin B combination would be good for you.'

He barely suppresses his sigh as he takes the sandwich. 'Thanks.'

'I have to go. Good luck if I don't see you before your interview tomorrow.'

'Cheers!' He holds up the sandwich like a toasting glass. 'Here's to the chance of a new start.'

I head off. When I get to the end of the path, I glance back. He's peeling open his sandwich and sniffing it. I sigh and hurry off to school.

'Morning, Agatha.'

'Morning, Liam.'

He hands over the paper for the day. I look at the headline on the front page –

MAXWELL ARRESTED IN CONNECTION WITH LONDON TERROR

– and, in smaller writing underneath –

SCHOOLGIRL CREDITED WITH FOILING PLOT

I fold the paper back up – I don't want to read it just yet.

'How are you?' I ask.

'I'm good. Getting a bit freaked out by people staring at me.'

I glance around the playground and a dozen heads turn away, pretending they hadn't been looking at us. I smile.

'Might as well enjoy it while it lasts – we're celebrities.'

Liam smiles, then frowns at something over my shoulder. I turn round to see Sarah Rathbone. Her expression is icy.

'Hello, Oddball.'

'Hello, Sarah.' I smile.

Her lip curls into a snarl. I can tell that she's trying to make me feel uncomfortable, to scare me, but I'm not scared any more. I've seen worse things in the last few days than a grumpy rich girl. It must have dawned on her that I'm not going to be intimidated, because she changes tack.

'What an amazing adventure you've had,' she drawls.

I smile some more. 'Yes, it's been quite a week . . .'

'Well, I just wanted to say well done.' She narrows her eyes, smiling the fakest of smiles. 'I'm just so glad you *got away with it.*'

She turns and strides away.

'What the hell was that about?' someone asks by my shoulder. It's Brianna.

'I have no idea,' I say with a shrug, as the three of us watch her go.

'Well, if you want someone to switch her hairspray for whipped cream, just let me know.'

I grin. 'Thanks, Bri.'

'No worries.' She brushes her hair behind her ear. I notice she has several small loop earrings round the top of each ear – instead of the CC uniform of a single tasteful diamond in each lobe. She's wearing a leather biker jacket – all against school rules of course.

'You look . . . different,' I say.

She smiles cautiously.

'Thanks. I feel different.'

⊸○

School goes by quickly, and I get used to people whispering as I pass. Liam is nervous about the attention, while Brianna soaks it up. Adulation is nothing new to her, but this time it's nothing to do with a carefully posed selfie. Several times I hear her retelling the story of our escape through the sugar maze, to a crowd of sixth-form girls, and it becomes more fantastical each time. I raise my eyebrow, but she shrugs as though to say, *who's gonna know?* I walk by, keeping my smile to myself – I enjoy our story passing into legend.

The bell rings for the end of day and the end of

term. A cheer goes up from the class, and people are running for the door, not waiting for Mr Wynne's permission, stuffing books into bags as they go. I just sit there, not wanting to rush. Liam is next to me, carefully putting his mathematical protractors away in the right slots.

'What do you think it'll be like, when we come back after summer?' I ask him.

Liam thinks about it for a while. 'I dunno . . . I think it'll mostly be back to the way things were. People forget stuff pretty quickly.'

I nod.

'That's what I thought. And I was also thinking . . . I don't want things to go back to the way they were – not back to normal anyway.'

He smiles.

'Agatha, things will never be normal with you around. There'll be other mysteries to solve.'

I think about those words and feel a bit better.

'Thanks, Liam. And when there are, we can solve them together.'

⌐○

The sun is shining on my walk home through Hyde Park, but my mind is elsewhere, back in the cavern under the earth. So I'm surprised when Dad opens the door when I reach the cottage.

'Dad, what are you doing home?'

'I came back early – we have a visitor.'

For a moment, I imagine Maxwell, somehow out of police custody and holding Dad hostage. What if he's standing behind Dad, a gun to his back?

Dad catches my expression and laughs. 'It's all right, Aggie – it's the good sort of visitor. Come on.' I follow him through to the kitchen.

'Dorothy is a high-up officer from the Metropolitan Police – she came to say thanks to you in person.'

I gasp as I see Professor D'Oliveira sitting at our kitchen table, sipping tea from china cups. I didn't even know we owned any china – Dad has clearly pulled out all the stops for her. She sets down her cup as I enter and smiles at me.

'Miss Oddlow! You'll forgive me for not getting up – my joints don't move quite as smoothly as they used to. Too long in a desk job!'

While Dad busies himself making me a cup of tea, she takes my hand between both of hers and squeezes it warmly. 'I told your dad I was with the Met so he didn't ask too many questions. The Guild is eager to initiate you,' she whispers. 'We have much to thank you for.' As she lets go of my hand, I find a tiny locket in my palm. I flip it up and inside is a picture of a key – the symbol of the Guild. The professor winks at me, and I slip the locket into my skirt pocket.

'Does that mean I've been accepted?' I whisper back.

'For initial training, yes. If you pass the tests, you could become our youngest agent ever.'

'What about Liam? He's really good with computers.'

My request doesn't seem to surprise her.

'First things first. But I'm sure we could consider his application.'

Dad reappears with my mug and joins us at the table. We munch on chocolate Hobnobs and sip tea. As Dad and Professor D'Oliveira make small talk, I find myself zoning out, Changing Channel. Hercule stands over by the window. He turns to me.

'But what about this mysterious "he" Maxwell spoke of? And what really happened to your mum?' he asks.

'Exactly!' I reply.

'What's that, love?' says Dad, offering me another biscuit. I smile and take one. The scene in the kitchen is ordinary and comforting – so unlike my recent experiences – I almost feel uneasy.

Like Liam says, things will never be 'normal' again.

And I don't want them to be.

ACKNOWLEDGEMENTS

Special thanks to Joe Heap and Rosie Sandler who worked so hard on bringing Agatha to life in these pages. They were helped enormously by Sophie Hignett and the team at Tibor Jones Studio, including Landa Acevedo-Scott, Ana Boado, Mary Rodgers, Charlotte Maddox and Kevin Conroy Scott. Rachel Denwood and the rest of the team at HarperCollins, in particular Nick Lake, Samantha Swinnerton, Kerrie McIlloney and Ann-Janine Murtagh, are fun, clever and incredibly supportive. A special mention goes to Michelle Misra, who is just awesome.

Don't miss the second book in this exciting new super-sleuth series!

Agatha Oddlow's just stumbled across her next big case . . . a murder at the British Museum.

But as Agatha starts to dig beneath the surface she begins to suspect that a wider plot is afoot below London – a plot involving a disused Tube station, a huge fireworks display and five thousand tonnes of gold bullion.

Luckily, Agatha's on the trail . . .

Join Agatha Oddlow on her third adventure!

An assistant at the National Gallery has gone missing, but when Agatha begins investigating she uncovers a plot bigger than she could ever have imagined. Join Agatha as she travels throughout London, and into the very heart of the mystery . . .